Faith knew Cameron Stevenson was strong.

And she knew—having seen him in one of the worst situations a parent would ever find themselves in—that he could be incredibly gentle with his son.

Realizing that she was still staring after him, she felt her cheeks heat and glanced around, hoping nobody noticed her hovering there in the corridor like some gawking groupie.

The fact was, she knew certain things about Cameron and she was enormously curious to know more, and it wasn't *all* caused by the fact that her hormones had unfrozen with unseemly haste the first time she'd ever seen him.

But Cameron Stevenson was a family man, pure and simple. So it didn't matter what sort of effect he had on her.

She wasn't going down *that* road ever again.

Dear Reader,

Spring might be just around the corner, but it's not too late to curl up by the fire with this month's lineup of six heartwarming stories. Start off with *Three Down the Aisle*, the first book in bestselling author Sherryl Woods's new miniseries, THE ROSE COTTAGE SISTERS. When a woman returns to her childhood haven, the last thing she expects is to fall in love! And make sure to come back in April for the next book in this delightful new series.

Will a sexy single dad find *All He Ever Wanted* in a search-and-rescue worker who saves his son? Find out in Allison Leigh's latest book in our MONTANA MAVERICKS: GOLD RUSH GROOMS miniseries. The Fortunes of Texas are back, and you can read the first three stories in the brand-new miniseries THE FORTUNES OF TEXAS: REUNION, only in Silhouette Special Edition. The continuity launches with *Her Good Fortune* by Marie Ferrarella. Can a straitlaced CEO make it work with a feisty country girl who's taken the big city by storm? Next, don't miss the latest book in Susan Mallery's DESERT ROGUES ongoing miniseries, *The Sheik & the Bride Who Said No*. When two former lovers reunite, passion flares again. But can they forgive each other for past mistakes? Be sure to read the next book in Judy Duarte's miniseries, BAYSIDE BACHELORS. A fireman discovers his ex-lover's child is *Their Secret Son*, but can they be a family once again? And pick up Crystal Green's *The Millionaire's Secret Baby*. When a ranch chef lands her childhood crush—and tycoon—can she keep her identity hidden, or will he discover her secrets?

Enjoy, and be sure to come back next month for six compelling new novels, from Silhouette Special Edition.

All the best,

Gail Chasan
Senior Editor

Please address questions and book requests to:
Silhouette Reader Service
U.S.: 3010 Walden Ave., P.O. Box 1325, Buffalo, NY 14269
Canadian: P.O. Box 609, Fort Erie, Ont. L2A 5X3

All He Ever Wanted

ALLISON LEIGH

Silhouette

SPECIAL EDITION

Published by Silhouette Books

America's Publisher of Contemporary Romance

For Chris, Pam, Judy, Karen and Cheryl,
fellow "Gold Rush Groomers" and for Susan,
who kept us on track. It's been a pleasure!

Special thanks and acknowledgment are given to
Allison Leigh for her contribution to the
MONTANA MAVERICKS: GOLD RUSH GROOMS series.

SILHOUETTE BOOKS

ISBN 0-373-24664-1

ALL HE EVER WANTED

Visit Silhouette Books at www.eHarlequin.com

Printed in U.S.A.

Books by Allison Leigh

Silhouette Special Edition

Stay... #1170
The Rancher and the Redhead #1212
A Wedding for Maggie #1241
A Child for Christmas #1290
Millionaire's Instant Baby #1312
Married to a Stranger #1336
Mother in a Moment #1367
Her Unforgettable Fiancé #1381
The Princess and the Duke #1465
Montana Lawman #1497
Hard Choices #1561
Secretly Married #1591
Home on the Ranch #1633
The Truth About the Tycoon #1651
All He Ever Wanted #1664

*Men of the Double-C Ranch

ALLISON LEIGH

started early by writing a Halloween play that her grade-school class performed. Since then, though her tastes have changed, her love for reading has not. And her writing appetite simply grows more voracious by the day.

She has been a finalist in the RITA® Award and the Holt Medallion contests. But the true highlights of her day as a writer are when she receives word from a reader that they laughed, cried or lost a night of sleep while reading one of her books.

Born in Southern California, Allison has lived in several different cities in four different states. She has been, at one time or another, a cosmetologist, a computer programmer and a secretary. She has recently begun writing full-time after spending nearly a decade as an administrative assistant for a busy neighborhood church, and currently makes her home in Arizona with her family. She loves to hear from her readers, who can write to her at P.O. Box 40772, Mesa, AZ 85274-0772.

Thunder Canyon, MT.
Population: 10,000
(Fictitious)

Chapter One

"How long has it been since you last saw your son?"

Cameron Stevenson eyed the police officer. Impatience clawed at him. He wanted to be out *looking* for Erik, not answering Bobby Romano's incessant questions. "Almost two hours. The band was taking their second break."

The officer's pencil scratched on his small notepad. "How do you know it was their second? Maybe it was their first. Their last."

Romano's neck was looking more appealing by the minute and Cam's hands itched to strangle it. But it wasn't Romano's fault that Erik was missing.

It was Cam's.

So instead of throttling the officer for detaining

him when he would otherwise have been scouring the buildings surrounding the Thunder Canyon Town Hall—usually known as The Hall—Cameron's fist tightened around the leather coat that Laura had given him their first winter together in Thunder Canyon.

Their only winter.

"It was Montana Gold's second break," he said flatly. "As soon as I saw the band members putting down their instruments, I started hunting for Erik. He'd already messed with the instruments after the band's first set. I didn't want him getting into mischief on the stage again." The first time, Erik's focus had been the drum set. The end result had been a crash of cymbals when the hi-hat tumbled off the stage. "It was around eight. I was gonna take him home."

Romano scratched his jaw and then made a few more notes. "And you're sure he's not just hiding? We all know how Erik can get. Kid was probably bored out of his skull coming to a wedding and reception."

Since it seemed as if everyone in town had crammed into The Hall to celebrate with the bridal couple—Katie Fenton and Justin Caldwell—Cam couldn't have very well come to the event without his son. None of the regular baby-sitters had been available. So he'd dragged Erik—not quite kicking and screaming—along with him.

Now he wished they both had stayed home. He hadn't wanted to come to the wedding in the first place, but Katie had been pretty insistent.

And he'd had the notion that Laura was standing behind him, silently pushing him to take part in the town's activities. So he'd accepted the invitation, and he'd lassoed Erik into accompanying him.

"He's not just hiding," he assured. The door to The Hall opened yet again, letting in a spit of snow along with the arrival. The evening had not only marked a second wedding for Katie to Justin in as many months, but it seemed to be capped by another blizzard as well.

Which only thinned out his control to a translucent veneer.

Most of the wedding guests had already departed because of the weather. Many of them were even now out looking for his son *despite* the weather.

While he was stuck in the lobby of the town hall answering Romano's damn questions.

"How do you know?" Romano was plodding.

Cam exhaled roughly. His fingers flexed. Tightened on the coat. "Because Rhonda Culpepper was here at the wedding, too." Rhonda manned the information desk for The Hall. She knew every nook and cranny of the place. "She had her keys. We checked all the offices upstairs. We checked the archives in the basement. We checked the damn elevator shaft. We checked every damn hiding hole in this entire damn place!" His voice rose, and there was little he could do to stop it. He towered over Romano, wanting to smash the man for hindering him.

"Here." A hand, holding a cup of water, appeared from one side, pushing between him and the police officer. A physical barrier. He looked at the cup for a moment, and the slender hand—then at the woman who'd offered it.

Faith Taylor.

He knew her only by sight.

Which was more than he wanted…and not because he didn't like the look of her.

He just didn't like the effect she had on him.

But she was SAR. Search and Rescue. The fact that his son might need her, though, or any other member of the county-wide team, made that veneer of control even thinner.

Don't panic.

"I don't want any water. I don't want to answer any more questions about how tall Erik is, or what he was wearing." Questions from Romano that had eroded Cam's nerves and pulverized his ability to remain calm. "I want to find my son. He's probably playing down on Main Street somewhere. He likes pretending he's an outlaw from the Old West."

"And the old-fashioned Western buildings all along Main provide the perfect setting." Faith's voice was calm enough. "Let's just hope that he's doing exactly that. And if he is, he'll be found quickly enough. There are officers and volunteers right now out canvassing the area, doing a door-to-door."

"And I should be out there with them. It's only getting later and that snow doesn't look like it's gonna lighten up anytime soon."

Her soft lips pressed together. Earlier in the evening, she'd worn a deep blue dress that had flowed around her slender ankles whenever she took a step. But since word had gotten out that Erik was missing, she'd changed. Now, she wore a coat similar to the one

Bobby Romano wore, only hers didn't bear the insignia of the Thunder Canyon police. It shouted Search and Rescue in nauseatingly bright orange letters across the back of the slick green fabric. She looked official.

Except for her eyes.

But looking at those eyes that were neither brown nor green but somewhere…distracting…in between was something he'd tried to avoid since the first time he'd seen her months ago sitting quietly in the rear of one of the town council meetings.

"Have you called your son's friends? Would he have tried walking home without you?"

"Erik tries anything," he said grimly. Despite Cam's concerted efforts otherwise. "And yes, I've called all of his friends. Most of the families were already here anyway."

There must have been three hundred people crowded into The Hall. And if Cam hadn't been cornered by the troublesome threesome—a term he'd privately applied to the trio of high school girls who were forever trying to practice their budding wiles on him—he'd have never lost sight of Erik in the first place.

"Yet you didn't call in the police right away," Romano observed. "Any particular reason for that, Coach?"

Cam narrowed his eyes. He didn't care for Romano's tone. He didn't care for Romano, for that matter. "Maybe because I was combing every square inch of this building, because I figured Erik *was* just hiding out. Only he's not. He's not *in* this building. Get it?"

He looked down at the coat his wife had given him.

God.

He couldn't lose Erik, too.

He shoved his arms into the coat.

Don't panic.

"I'm going to find my son."

He ignored Romano and Faith and turned on his heel. His boots rang out hollow on the wood floor of the nearly empty lobby and the wind ripped the door out of his grip when he stepped onto the wooden side-walk outside the entrance. The awning that stretched across the front of The Hall, as well as the adjacent buildings butting up against it, didn't offer much protection against the swirl of snow.

He flipped up his collar and set off across the street. The town square held plenty of hiding places for a seven-year-old boy. "Erik," he yelled, his feet moving faster.

He shouldn't have made Erik go to the wedding and reception. Shouldn't have made him put on his best clothes—even a damned tie. His son had been nearly apoplectic.

Rightfully so, Cam had realized, as soon as they'd walked into The Hall and had seen just how casually many of the guests were dressed, given the short notice of Katie and Justin's "do." Erik had slanted a look up at Cam and immediately started fiddling with his tie, despite Cam's warning. Ten minutes later, he'd caught his son in the bathroom, wrapping toilet paper around his head like a turban. The turban had been ditched, but the tie had come off and Erik had returned to his seat with Cam.

"Erik!"

He rounded a slow-moving car and nearly hurdled an old-fashioned bench sitting outside a Western-themed storefront.

Don't panic.

"Mr. Stevenson. Wait."

He very nearly ignored the raised voice. But he stopped, impatience coiling inside him, and turned to see Faith Taylor jogging across the road, her sturdy boots kicking up puffs of snow.

"Don't mind Bobby." She skidded a little on the slippery road as she reached him. "He really is trying to help."

Cam steadied her and just as quickly released her. "He's pissed that I've still got his son benched," he said bluntly. Danny Romano—Romance, as he was called—was one of the strongest players on the high school basketball team Cam coached. He was also carrying the worst grades. But that didn't matter to his dad, Bobby, who was more interested in his son being spotted by a scout than whether or not his son had decent enough grades to even be accepted into college.

Faith's long blond hair—confined in a ponytail—rippled and lifted in the harsh wind, reflecting the dim glow from a nearby lamppost. "He's going back to the police station to make the report. A broadcast will go out on the local television station. Did you have a picture to give him?"

Cam nodded, his gaze scanning the white-dark shadows of the town square. He could hear the shouts of his son's name, and through the swirling snow, could see the bob of flashlights. "Erik's school picture." It had been in his wallet, next to the photo of Laura when she'd been pregnant.

"Good. The more people who see it, the better. The radio station here will also be making the announcement. And there's no one who might have taken Erik? Your wife, or—"

"My wife is dead. And there are no other family members in the area."

Her lips parted for the briefest moment. "I'm sorry. I, um, I didn't know that." She hesitated, as if she were adjusting her thought processes. "I assume Bobby told you the process for issuing an AMBER alert?"

He nodded. The very notion of a nationwide alert being issued for his missing son was more than he could stand, because it would mean that Erik hadn't just wandered off. It would mean that his son had been abducted. That he could be facing serious injury. Or death.

His head felt ready to explode.

Don't panic.

How many times had he issued that advice to Laura?

Erik would be fine. He was probably sitting in someone's living room, drinking hot chocolate and talking about the impossibility of two snowflakes being identical as he watched them hurtle from the sky.

"Okay. Well, we're not at that point, which is a good thing." She shifted from one foot to the other, her legs looking long and slender in her heavy, tan pants. "I'll head out in just a few minutes, too. I've been in contact with the other members of my team. Unfortunately, thanks to this snow, it'll be a while before any of them can make it here to Thunder Canyon. And, of course, while the search is still confined to the town limits, the police are in charge of coordinating the search."

"Erik is still in town," he said. Because he had to believe it.

"You're probably right," she agreed evenly. "And you need to go home. It's likely that your son will show up there."

She clearly didn't know Erik. "He won't."

"Mr. Stevenson—"

"Cam."

She exhaled in a visible puff. "Mr. Stevenson. Let us do *our* job. Go home."

"What you really mean is that you don't think I've done *my* job," he countered.

Another gust of wind blew over them and she flipped up the lined collar of her coat, deftly fastening it around her neck. She didn't deny his words, either. "Let's just find Erik," she said. "The quicker the better, considering the way this storm is picking up. Has he run off like this before?"

"No. Yes." He shook his head sharply. "Dammit. I have to find him. This is wasting more—"

"Don't." She touched her gloved hand to his sleeve. "I know you're worried. Upset. But the best thing that you can do is try to stay calm, and go home. Make a list of Erik's friends. The places he likes to go. Was he upset about anything? Did you argue?"

"Being forced into a monkey suit," Cam muttered.

"And Erik doesn't run off because he's angry. He runs off because he sees a bug he's interested in, or a rabbit he wants to follow. He's seven. He's got more energy and curiosity than either one of us knows what to do with." Attention deficit wasn't his son's problem, either. He just had an insatiable curiosity toward life.

In that regard, he was like Laura.

And Cam hadn't been able to protect Laura.

He *would* protect their son.

If he could only find him.

"Okay." Faith nodded. "So go home. Call the station and give them just that kind of information once you're there. And wait for Erik."

"I'll do better looking."

"But—"

"I've already told Todd Gilmore to go over to my place in case Erik shows," he interrupted. "The Gilmores live next door to me." Todd was the star center on the team. He was also one of the more reliable students at Thunder Canyon High School where Cam taught math and coached the men's athletic teams—football, basketball and baseball, depending on the season.

The information didn't seem to please Faith Taylor any, though. She still looked at him with something not quite veiled in her expression.

Judgment.

Well, nobody could judge Cam more harshly than he judged himself and he wasn't going to stand there—useless—on that cold sidewalk any longer. "I appreciate whatever help you can give." He pushed out the words, meaning them. He just didn't like having to mean them.

Asking for—or accepting—help from others didn't sit comfortably on his shoulders.

But when it came to Erik, Cam would do whatever it took.

Faith shoved her gloved hands in her pockets and watched Cameron Stevenson turn on his booted heel. In moments, his tall body seemed swallowed by the swirling, snowy shadows filling the darkened town square. There was no point in trying to call him back. Or to ask him to wait.

The truth was, Erik Stevenson probably *would* be located quickly enough—right here in this old section of Thunder Canyon—now that folks knew to keep an eye out for the boy. It was a far more likely scenario than that the child had met with any foul play.

Even though Thunder Canyon possessed a population of ten thousand, the crime rate was so low it was nearly nonexistent.

She chewed the inside of her lip. Closed her eyes for a moment when she heard Cameron Stevenson's deep voice calling his son's name.

If she were lucky enough to have a son, she wouldn't be so careless as to lose sight of him.

And that was a thought that wouldn't lead anywhere but to depression. So she opened her eyes, dashing snowflakes away from her eyelashes, and headed back to her SUV, which she'd left double-parked in front of the brightly lit town hall.

She climbed in and drove as quickly as the weather

permitted back to her office at the fire station. She'd make yet another attempt at raising another member of the SAR team, but she had no plans to sit on her thumbs if she couldn't. There were only six of them on the team, and they covered the entire county. It was only on rare occasions that they were all called in to one case at one time.

Erik Stevenson probably *would* be located safe and sound somewhere nearby. And she'd be one of the people out looking for him, until he was home again with his father.

And maybe next time, Cameron Stevenson would keep his thick-lashed brooding brown eyes more clearly focused on his innocent little boy.

When she reached the public service building, a big brick complex that housed both the Thunder Canyon police and fire departments, she parked in her usual spot and hurried inside, grateful to get out of the bitter wind.

She didn't have an office assigned for her use in the portion of the building used by the fire department, but had a serviceable metal desk, a few filing cabinets and a computer, all situated off to one side of the open office area. She yanked off her coat and sat down at her desk, then dialed her co-workers' numbers with one hand and punched up her computer with the other.

A grainy image of young Erik Stevenson immediately came up and for a moment she sat there, looking into his impossibly young face.

He looked like a miniature version of his dad, right down to the squarely cut jaw, dark auburn hair and deep brown eyes. For a moment, she wondered if Cameron would have the same cowlick that Erik possessed if his hair weren't cut so conservatively short.

"Hey there, Blondie." Derek Winters, one of the members of Fire's C Company and the husband of her best friend, Tanya, tugged at the end of her ponytail and sat on the corner of her desk. "Any news on the Stevenson kid?"

"Not yet."

"He's a cute one." He jerked his chin toward the small television that sat atop one of the tall filing cabinets across the room. "His picture's been all over the news for the past thirty minutes."

"Good." She gave up on the phone and quickly typed out a report and posted it to the county system where the rest of her team could access the information. "The more exposure, the better."

"Well, talking about exposure—" Derek's face looked serious "—the weather service has issued a severe weather alert for the next seven hours. They're expecting road closures all the way to Bozeman."

Dismay settled cold and heavy inside her. "The father said Erik has his parka and gloves with him." Which would be sufficient under *normal* circumstances. She propped her elbows on her desk and pressed her chin to her linked fingers, sternly marshalling her thoughts. "I've heard that a lot of people think this boy is pretty mischievous." She looked up at Derek. "What was Toby like when he was seven?" Her honorary nephew was now twelve.

Derek's lips curled. "Hell on wheels one minute.

Too angelic for belief the next." He shook his head. "If I were in Cam Stevenson's position right now, I'd be ready to rip apart the whole world until I knew my kid was safe."

Which pretty much described Faith's impression of Cameron Stevenson's state of mind.

She rose and grabbed her coat again. She had spare gloves and scarves in her truck. She checked the batteries in her flashlight and took a freshly charged radio from the row of them on the rear counter. "Cam spent half the evening at the reception tonight surrounded by women." She wasn't sure what made her admit the observation. It wasn't as if she'd sat at the table alongside Tanya watching the man the entire while.

Derek was grinning. "Poor guy. We can't all be beautiful like me. And it doesn't mean that he wasn't watching his kid properly," he added more seriously.

Faith couldn't make a call on that particular point, no matter which way she instinctively leaned. All she knew was that the few times she'd seen Cameron Stevenson since she'd returned to Thunder Canyon last year, he'd almost always had a bevy of females flocking around him. Didn't matter if it was at a town council meeting, where he often posed incredibly pointed questions to the council members, or at The Hitching Post for hamburgers and shakes following a Friday night high school ball game.

She could understand why the man wouldn't take a child to a council meeting. But she hadn't yet seen Erik in The Hitching Post following one of the games.

Maybe Cameron Stevenson did watch his son properly.

And maybe he didn't.

She'd barely seen the boy amid the mad crush attending Katie and Justin's wedding.

"I'm going out. The rest of the search is concentrated around Old Town. It's unlikely that he would have gone so far, but I told Romano that I'd check out White Water Drive and the houses down that way. Then I'll work my way around the edge of town and up Thunder Canyon Road."

"You think he could have headed out to the ice rink?"

She shook her head. "A unit already checked it out. He wasn't there. And he hasn't been seen on Lazy-D property, either." The ranch owned by the prosperous Douglas family bordered the entire western side of town.

She waved the radio in her hand and headed out the door. The snow was steady. Her SUV was already coated in white. She swiped her arm across the windshield as far as she could reach and then climbed inside. The heater blasted warm and comforting almost immediately as she backed out of her space and drove slowly through the town where she'd been born and raised. She hoped to heaven that Erik was somewhere warm.

As she drove, she could see the steady track of Thunder Canyon police vehicles moving carefully up and down the streets.

Wherever Erik Stevenson had gotten to, they *would* find him.

She refused to even consider the alternative.

She drove back up Main Street, past the town square and The Hall. When she reached White Water Drive, she turned south. Drove past the hospital, where her brother Chris was probably still on duty in the E.R.

The farther out she went, the heavier the snow seemed to fall, until her SUV was virtually crawling. She'd flipped on both her spotlights, but the powerful beams went only so far through the wall of white. When she reached the last of the houses, a little past the Lone Pine Medical Building, she got out and started door-to-door, working her way back up toward the hospital. When she reached it, she took a few precious minutes to grab a hot coffee from the cafeteria. She also radioed in to the station.

Still no news.

And now, it was nearly midnight.

There was a steady chatter coming from the police scanner in her SUV. Officers reporting in. The search grids of the town being slowly and steadily ticked off, yielding no sign of Erik.

She continued her way back toward the center of Old Town—driving a few feet, knocking on doors, waking people up, tramping around their houses, their yards, calling Erik's name, only to drive a few more feet and repeat the process. It was freezing, tedious work, but she never once gave a thought to stopping.

At twelve-thirty, the snow picked up even more, but it was hardly noticeable since the wind had also picked up, throwing whatever fell right back up again and swirling it around twice as hard. She ignored the command over the scanner that all searchers were to seek immediate shelter from the blizzard.

And when those commands were directed squarely at her, she turned off the scanner and still continued. She didn't take her orders from the police. She took them from the senior member of the search and rescue team, and *he* was over in Bozeman.

Not that Jim Shepherd would be pleased with her when he found out, but she couldn't get the image of Erik's face out of her head.

She'd grown up in this town. She'd learned to drive on its streets. And when it came to Old Town, she knew every corner like the back of her hand. So as long as she could still make her way from one house to the next, she was going to.

Which was fine, until she nearly drove her crawling truck right over the figure hunched against the wind outside The Hitching Post.

She sat there in her truck, her gloved hands curling tightly around the steering wheel as she stared at the person barely a foot from her front bumper.

There was no question who it was.

Erik's father.

The wind buffeted the SUV, and Cameron swayed.

She shoved the truck into Park, grabbed the blanket from her back seat and raced around to him, her boots sliding on the ice. Reaching up, she yanked the blanket around his shoulders.

"Are you crazy?" Her raised voice, muffled by her scarf and whipped away by the wind, was barely audible. The man was stiff with cold, his leather coat no match for the elements. "You're not supposed to be out here still!"

His head ducked toward hers. "*You* are!"

Bitter wind shot needles of cold into her, nearly shoving her off her feet. She grabbed his waist, as much to keep herself steady as him. "Get in the truck," she yelled.

He was already moving, and she wasn't sure if she pushed him or if he pulled her. He went to the passenger door. Dragged it open, and nearly lifted her inside. He was close behind, the door slamming closed on them.

The protection from that awful, bitter wind was immediate and she blew out a long breath.

"Jesus," he muttered, as the air howled and the SUV rocked. From the glow of the dashboard, his eyes looked ravaged. "You haven't found him, either."

She wanted to look away from those eyes of his. Wanted to, but couldn't.

And she loathed the feeling that engulfed her.

Failure.

She wasn't used to it in her professional life.

Personal? That was a different story.

So she stared up at him, unconsciously cataloging the creases—deeper now than they'd been hours earlier—that fanned out from his eyes.

"No," she said quietly. "Not yet." She was half perched on the console between the seats, half perched on his thigh, and she awkwardly maneuvered herself into the driver's seat, anxious to put some distance between them.

She tried closing herself off from the desperation seeping from him and turned on the scanner again, only to hear her name being furiously called. She lifted the mike and reported in.

Beside her, Cameron was still. He had to have been freezing, but he didn't pull the blanket tighter around himself, or redirect the heater vents more in his direction.

Sighing faintly, she leaned over again, pulling the blanket around him more fully, then simply reached even further to grab his safety belt and snap it in place.

She squeezed his arm. "We'll find him," she whispered.

His jaw worked and when his voice finally emerged, it was raw.

"When?"

Chapter Two

When?

Faith slowly sat back in her seat. "Soon," she promised, her voice husky.

The station was just as close as trying to get either one of them home. And at the station, there was still some hope that she'd be able to do some good where little Erik Stevenson was concerned.

Closer or not, her nerves were strung tighter than a wire and her eyes ached by the time her tires slid to a wobbly stop outside the fire station. She felt as if she'd been driving for hours, but knew it had been a fraction of it.

Outside her windshield, beyond the frenzied slap of the wipers, she could just make out the familiar brick wall of the public service building. "Can you make it inside?" She handed him her spare scarf.

He didn't answer. Merely wound it around his neck and face, and shoved himself out of the vehicle.

She pulled her own scarf up higher around her nose and followed suit, heading straight for the wall that was made elusive by the undulating curtain of snowfall.

When her gloved hands hit solid surface, she didn't dawdle with relief, but ducked her head even more against the vicious wind and felt her way along the wall until she found the entrance. Cameron's shoulder brushed hers all the while.

The wind nearly picked them up and tossed them inside.

Breathing hard, she sat down on the nearest object. The floor.

Cameron folded his arms across the top of a tall filing cabinet. His head bowed wearily, and the blanket fell from his shoulders, unheeded. After a long moment, he shrugged out of his coat and placed it with inordinate care over the back of a desk chair.

She sat there, still trying to catch her breath while sympathy shoved hard against the knot inside her that wanted to blame him for being careless with his child.

She looked away from him, unwinding her heavy scarf. It crunched as chunks of snow and ice fell from it, only to melt when they rained onto the floor.

She leaned her head back. Felt the unyielding metal of a desk drawer behind her. And wanted to rail at the weather gods for throwing the nastiest of curveballs their way.

"Here." Cam crouched down before her and began tugging off her thick gloves. He said nothing else.

His expression was enough to let her know where his thoughts dwelled.

She looked like the abominable snowman, and he wasn't much better. And his son was still missing.

Cameron Stevenson was a big man with shoulders that had undoubtedly filled a football uniform at some point in his past. Not brawny. But definitely muscular. Strong.

She had the impossible urge to put her arms around him as if he were a harmless child nursing a hurt.

She swallowed hard, until she got rid of the knot in her throat that would do nobody any good right now.

"The weather will ease up," she assured, her voice not quite as calm as she'd have preferred. "We'll all go back out again."

His jaw was white. He rose and his movements were slow, as if moving caused him pain. He began to pace.

Her iced-over pants had thawed sufficiently thanks to the warm interior of the building, and she pushed to her feet as well. She went back to the locker room and changed into the spare clothes she kept there. She wouldn't win any fashion awards, but the olive-drab cargo pants and fleece sweatshirt were warm and dry.

She returned to her desk, giving Cameron—whose expression was closed and unwelcoming—a wide berth. He'd exchanged the well-cut black suit he'd been wearing when she'd seen him at The Hall for a thick gray sweater and blue jeans. A dark shadow blurred his blunt jaw and his hair looked as if it had been raked by claws. His tension, however, *was* terribly familiar. Only now it was worse.

She checked her computer, amazed to find the Internet connection still running.

But there was no news about Erik there, either. No sightings. And no help from any other members of her team coming anytime soon, since the roads had officially been closed and they were dealing with their own local emergencies.

Stifling a sigh, she crossed the hallway that divided the building and went over to the police station. There were a handful of officers sitting at their desks, looking busy. All except Bobby Romano, who was leaning back in his chair, his boots propped on the corner of his desk.

The sight irritated her.

She went over to him and shoved his feet off the desk.

"Hey!" The cup of coffee he held splashed over his uniformed stomach. "What the hell?"

"At least pretend to be on duty, Bobby." Her voice was flat. She ignored the muffled snickers coming from the others and went past his desk to the dispatcher's office.

When she stuck her head in, she saw that Cheryl Lansky held the fort. "I'm here. You can call off the dogs."

"Taking chances, Faith." Cheryl tsked and shook her head. "I'll let the chief know you've come in, though."

"I nearly ran down Cameron Stevenson," she admitted. "Any reports?"

"Aside from the usual panics over a blizzard, only call we've gotten is the weekly from Emelda Ross."

Bobby came up behind Faith, sopping at his shirt with a paper towel. "Woman needs to be put in a home somewhere."

Cheryl looked disgusted.

"Is she still doing the story hour at the library?" Faith asked.

Cheryl nodded. "My grandson loves her just as much as his mother did."

"She told the best stories," Faith murmured. "But what'd she call in for tonight?"

"Same thing she calls in for every week," Bobby grumbled. He tossed the soaked towel in the small metal wastebasket beside Cheryl's desk and her array of computers, phones and radios, and missed. "Attention."

Cheryl leaned over and deposited the trash where it belonged. "Suspected trespasser." She shrugged a little. "Same complaint she always makes."

"Did someone check it out?" Faith looked at Bobby.

"We did a drive-by, before the storm settled in after the Coach decided to announce his kid was missing," he defended. "That old house of hers was quiet as a tomb. There isn't gonna be any trespassers going anywhere tonight. Not with that white soup coming down out there."

"And don't you go thinking you're going back out in this storm yet, either, Faith." Cheryl's voice was firm. She might smooth things over with the chief on Faith's behalf, but she was drawing a line. "I'll let you know if anything useful comes in."

It would have to do. Faith nodded. "Thanks."

"Been compiling the results of the search areas," Bobby told her grudgingly. "Copy of the report for you is in the folder on my desk."

Faith nodded. It was strictly courtesy that had him giving her the report, and she was glad that she hadn't had to wrangle it out of him. She picked up the folder on her way back to her own work area.

Instead of pacing, Cameron was now sitting by her desk, staring at the faint specks of color in the serviceable tile beneath his squarely planted boots.

She slid into her desk chair and flipped open the folder, scanning the results of the police search. The tension emanating from Cam was palpable.

On the television screen across the room the blurb about the missing boy was being repeated. Erik's engaging grin gleamed out from the small screen. Then a snowy shot of volunteers searching, including many members of Cameron Stevenson's own basketball team. The jolting, bouncing video showed them going door-to-door, canvassing the town, before the weather had been deemed too dangerous for anyone's efforts.

She looked back to see Cameron, his thumb and forefinger digging into his closed eyes.

"Why don't you try and get some sleep," she suggested softly.

His lips twisted. "Right."

Since she wouldn't be able to sleep in his position either, she dropped it.

The last thing she wanted to do was finish up paperwork, but she forced herself through the motions. The minutes ticked by. Excruciatingly slow.

Please, God, let that boy be somewhere safe and warm.

The knot in her stomach wouldn't let her find comfort in the silent plea.

Cameron rose again. Paced. Cursed. He moved from the fire department side to the police department side, and in his absence Faith propped her elbows on her desk and raked back her hair, struggling against the worst of the thoughts they'd all been willing Cameron Stevenson not to even think. And when he returned, she had herself once more under control while he paced some more. Made phone calls. Stared hard out the window.

"Is it still snowing?"

"Can't tell." He pressed his palm against the wind-rattled windowpane for a moment.

No matter what she did or didn't think about him, the action broke her heart.

"The sun will be up soon."

"If it breaks through the clouds."

"Don't lose hope, Mr. Stevenson. The sun always comes out eventually."

His face was tight when he turned and looked at her. "If that's a metaphor that my son will be found, save it."

"It's a simple fact," she said evenly. "With daylight, we'll resume the search."

"How many missing kids have you found?"

"Enough." And then, because she didn't want him asking if all of them had been found unharmed, she turned back to her desk and started shuffling papers together. When her telephone rang, she started.

Cam's dark gaze crawled from the ringing telephone to Faith's face. She swallowed and lifted the receiver. "Taylor."

It was Cheryl. But as soon as the dispatcher mentioned that she was calling about Emelda Ross, Faith's shoulders relaxed. Lowered.

From the corner of her eye, she saw Cameron's hands curl into fists, then slowly, deliberately relax.

She'd dealt with a lot of families and friends who were concerned when someone they cared about went missing…on a hike, while camping, while rock hunting. Something about Cam's worry hit her in a spot she tried hard to keep under wraps. What good was a search-and-rescue worker too emotionally wrought to do her job?

She smoothed back her hair. Murmured some excuse and crossed the hall again. Ignored Romano and stuck her head in Cheryl's office once more.

"What exactly did Miss Emelda say?"

"Listen for yourself." Cheryl had the recording already queued up. "Think the poor woman is as nervous as a cat with the storm. Weather service said the front is moving out more quickly than they'd expected though. That's good news."

Miss Emelda's voice didn't sound particularly frail or frightened to Faith. What she sounded was mighty irritated at the lack of attention her *first* call had received.

When the recording finished, Cheryl just looked at her with a shrug. "Romano wasn't exaggerating. She calls in every week like clockwork."

"Where does she live?"

Cheryl leaned over and tapped the large map of Thunder Canyon that was affixed to her wall. "Same place as always. Don't know why she doesn't move to one of the newer homes in town considering how many nervous calls she puts in to us. But she's still in that sprawling old place out past Elk."

Faith eyed the map. Emelda Ross's home was located on the western outskirts of town. The only thing further out than her place was the ice rink and Douglas property. Her gaze traced along the road, backtracking toward town. Cheryl hadn't been given a chance to ask the elderly woman about Erik during the second phone call, because Miss Emelda hadn't let her get in a word edgewise.

"What did Romano say? About Miss Emelda calling again?"

"I haven't told him." Cheryl's lips pursed. "You know what he'd say. Fact is, though, the whole squad is benched 'cause of the blizzard and this was a nonemergency call. If she were really scared, she'd have better luck complaining of shortness of breath, because we'd dispatch a fire unit out to her, and she knows that."

Faith fiddled with the sturdy watch she wore, still studying the map. Emelda Ross's house was barely in the town limits. But as the crow flew, it was definitely within walking distance of The Hall. Question was, whether or not it was walking distance for young Erik. "But *I* could go out there."

"If Erik Stevenson somehow found his way from The Hall to Miss Emelda's place, she would have said so in her call."

Cheryl was only saying what Faith was already thinking. "Yes. I know."

"The snowplows haven't been out yet. The roads are impassible."

"I'll take the snowmobile. You can break the news to Romano if you'd like."

Cheryl's lips quirked. "My pleasure." There was little that Cheryl enjoyed more than needling the officer. He barely tolerated Faith's presence. Cooperated with her only because the Chief would come down on him if he didn't. But he never liked the notion that Faith and her team accomplished anything that the police didn't.

Glancing at the big wall map one more time, Faith crossed the hall again and quickly nixed the half-formed notion of asking Cameron if he wanted to go with her.

He was sitting beside her desk again, still as a sigh, his arms folded tightly over his chest.

He was asleep.

She was glad Derek and the other members of Company C were all snoozing, some in the sleeping quarters of the building, some sprawled on the massive recliners crowded into the station's recreation room.

Because without the fire crew present, she didn't have to worry about anyone noticing the way her feet dragged to a halt, or her hand pressed hard to her chest for a moment.

There was something wrong with her in that she was somewhat undone by the sight of that tense father finally dozing.

Moving quietly, she keyed in a report of her plans to her team and collected a fresh radio and the keys to one of the snowmobiles that were garaged in a smaller building on the other side of the parking lot. She went back to the locker room and added a pair of thermal underwear beneath her clothes, then bundled up in her coat and gloves again.

Outside, the wind was still blowing, but not quite as severely. And the snow *had* stopped. Visibility was considerably improved. Still, there was no way she'd be able to maneuver her SUV through the drifts of snow filling the streets. She unlocked the garage housing the small fleet of snowmobiles and other off-road equipment. Minutes later, the whine of the engine filled the odd quiet, and she slowly steered the massive machine out of the lot.

There was no point worrying about the roads, so she went south, then west, cutting across snowy fields and empty lots in a sloppy, loose arc. When she got to Thunder Canyon Road, she dropped down into the ditch that ran alongside it. The headlight gleamed ahead of her in a wide sweep and she opened the throttle.

The powerful cat sped over the thick powder and

in minutes she'd made it to Miss Emelda's ancient home. Tucking her radio in her lapel pocket, she approached the house. Before she'd even reached the steps, the front porch light snapped on and the door creaked open. "Who's there?"

Faith's boots crunched to a stop in the snow. "Miss Emelda? It's Faith Taylor. Cheryl Lansky told me you called in again and I just wanted to come by and make sure you were all right."

"All right?" The woman pushed the door wider and Faith saw the business end of a shotgun slowly lower, to be enfolded by yards of flower-sprigged flannel and a dark, calf-length coat. "Of course I'm all right. Not that those idiots down at the police station—who can't find their way out of a paper bag, mind you—care whether or not I am. Well, come on up, girl. You're probably half-frozen."

She wasn't, but she went up the steps anyway, then stomped the snow off her boots before entering. Miss Emelda was locking the shotgun in a glass-fronted gun display. "Should know better than to call the police," she said when she turned. "Bunch of young pups, thinking I'm just a lonely old woman jumping at shadows." She waved her hand toward the chintz couch. "Sit down. Sit down."

Faith reluctantly sat. "Miss Emelda, perhaps you could—"

"Do you still read the classics?" The elderly woman settled herself on a chair with crocheted antimacassars covering the arms. Judging by the ball of thread and long needle on the coffee table, Miss

Emelda had crocheted the delicate arm coverings herself.

"I...excuse me?"

"The classics, girl. You were reading Dumas before any other child in your class."

"The Man in the Iron Mask," Faith murmured. "I'm surprised you remember that."

"Of course I remember." Miss Emelda smiled. "I remember all my children. And now you're back in Thunder Canyon despite the adventures you set off to find."

Adventures wasn't exactly the term Faith would have used to describe her time away from Thunder Canyon. "Well, I remember you talking about a lot of adventures during story hour at the library when I was little. Miss Emelda, what made you think you might have a trespasser out here last night?"

"Dog was going crazy." She raised her voice. "Dog!" A small Jack Russell terrier trotted into the room. "He doesn't bark unless someone's out in the yard."

Faith held out her hand for the curious dog. He gave her wrist an experimental sniff, then slopped his tongue over her fingers.

"He started barking before I heard your snowmobile," she said surely.

"Would you mind if I took a look around?"

Miss Emelda looked surprised. "Why would you want to do that? This was a job for the police. Like I told them. Someone wanted to break into my garage out back. My father's Model T is parked out there, you know. Only reason I called again is because Dog kept whining. I was afraid whoever it was might've gotten stuck in my garage from the storm."

Faith honestly wasn't certain what sort of market there was for stolen Model Ts, particularly in Thunder Canyon. And Miss Emelda undoubtedly did know better than anyone else whether or not her garage was being broken into. "Do you think it might be possible that it was Erik Stevenson, rather than a trespasser?"

"Erik? Good gracious, why would I think that?"

"He went missing from Katie's reception last night."

Miss Emelda pressed her hand to her chest, her delicately wrinkled visage fading. "Well…when? I saw him at The Hall with his daddy. He was as much a live wire as ever. The darling can hardly manage to sit still during story hour on Friday afternoons. Reminds me of your brother, Christopher, actually, when he was that age. Always asking questions. Wanting to know how things work. Such a shame what happened with his mother."

Now was not the time to indulge Faith's own insatiable curiosity. "I'd like to look around your property if you don't mind."

"Of course." Her hands fluttered. "Of course, dear, you do anything you want. Oh, my, that poor boy. I left the reception when the music first started playing. I'm afraid these ears are too old to acquire a taste for anything other than big band. How did I not know?"

"If you haven't had on your television or radio you wouldn't have," Faith murmured. Undoubtedly, Miss

Emelda wasn't the only one. And she could still hold out hope that Erik was snug as a bug in one of those households that hadn't been reached by the broadcasts, or the door-to-doors.

It was possible.

But unlikely, a worried voice whispered.

Faith headed to the door. Miss Emelda followed after her, her nightgown and coat flapping around her. "He's so curious," she fretted.

Faith was gaining a pretty detailed impression of young Erik. "That's what I hear." She smiled reassuringly at Miss Emelda as she pulled open the door. "Look. The sky is starting to lighten up already." It wasn't entirely an exaggeration. The sky had gone from pitch to a dark, charcoal gray.

"Well, you watch your step anyway," Miss Emelda called after her. "Particularly if you go out past the windmill at the edge of my property." She gestured at some distant point beyond her house. "The snow's likely to cover over any holes in the ground and there are still tunnels out there from the Queen of Hearts mine."

Faith froze for a moment, and it had nothing whatsoever to do with the frigid temperature. "The mine?" How could she have forgotten the Douglas's defunct gold mine?

"Played out almost before it began." Illuminated by the lights behind her, Emelda's white curls looked like a halo. "Folks tend to think the only thing left of it are memories and geegaws over at the museum. But the tunnels are still there. Ground's eroded in a few places.

Some holes are covered over. Some aren't. So you watch your step."

Faith nodded. "I'll be careful. It's cold. Stay inside."

Miss Emelda nodded and closed the door, her movements reluctant. Faith returned to the snowmobile and radioed in to Cheryl. Any minute, she knew the first rays of sunlight would start sending experimental fingers over the horizon. But for now, it was still dark. The wind still howled. And the air still smelled of snow.

The snowmobile cut a clean swath through the sea of snow as Faith steered it past Miss Emelda's house. She directed her powerful searchlight in a slow sweep. Whether Erik had been there or not, the snowstorm had obliterated whatever footprints might have been left behind.

She carefully circled the gabled garage. Tried to pull open the double door. There was a lot of play, but ultimately, the wide wooden doors stayed put. Still, she crouched down, peering through the separation. "Erik?"

She heard a soft shuffling and her nerves went into overdrive. She pulled out her penlight and directed the narrow beam of light through the opening, trying to make heads or tails of what she could see. "Erik, are you in there?"

She heard the crunch of snow, then felt a hand fall on her shoulder. She jerked around, tumbling onto her rear. Her penlight rolled out of her fingers and landed end-up in the snow, the narrow light shining up a long, denim-clad leg.

Her heart dropped out of her throat and returned to its usual spot in her chest as recognition settled. "Mr.

Stevenson. What are you doing here?" She couldn't believe she hadn't heard his truck, which she could see behind him. It looked as if it were half-stuck in the deep snow near the house. She thought about commenting on how dangerous the driving conditions were, but thought better of it.

He crouched down, plucking the penlight from the snow, and handed it to her. "I'm doing the same thing you are. Looking for my son. Cheryl Lansky told me you came out here." He pulled at the ancient wooden doors, the same way she had. "Erik? Come on, bud, if you're in there, it's time to come out."

But Faith realized that the only sounds she'd thought she'd heard hadn't come from the inside of the locked garage. They'd come from Cameron Stevenson. "He's not in there."

"Erik!"

Cameron pulled harder on the door and it groaned so violently, Faith feared the frozen hinges would pop right out of the wood. She pushed to her feet and closed her gloved hands around his arm. "Mr. Stevenson. Erik is *not* in the garage!"

Even through the layers of gloves, coats and sweaters, she could feel his muscles bunch. Could feel the resistance in him, the need to believe his son was so close. "We need to keep looking," she said quietly.

She could feel, more than see, his glare. By slow degrees, his grip on the doors eased. He let go, and the wood all but sighed in relief as the door settled.

"I can't lose him, too." His voice was barely audible, yet its rawness tore at her.

Her fingers curled against the thickness of his coat. "You can't give up."

His voice dropped even lower. "It's been more than ten hours."

She was well aware of that. Painfully so.

Maybe the man hadn't watched his son properly, but he was suffering now.

Then her radio crackled with life and she started just as badly as he did. But it was just Cheryl, dispatching a fire unit out to a woman in labor.

The noise was enough to rally her focus away from the father back to the boy, where it belonged. "I don't suppose it'll do me any good to tell you to go inside with Miss Emelda." She looked pointedly at his truck. "You could call for a tow truck to pull that loose, and then *go home.*"

He shook his head.

"Then come with me." She tugged her knitted cap down around her ears and mounted the snowmobile again. When he climbed on behind her, taking up more than his share of the seat, she closed her mind off to everything but Erik. She headed out toward the stark windmill that seemed little more than a skeletal shadow against the sky, as it turned ever so slowly in the still morning.

She pulled up next to it, and cut her engine. The silence was overwhelming.

"What are you doing?"

She tilted her head, closing her eyes, concentrating on the silence. Had she heard something? "Listening."

The only thing answering her was a soft creak from

the windmill. She turned off the searchlight and pulled out the penlight. When she started to tuck it between her teeth, he took it from her and directed it at the map she spread out.

"What are we looking for?" His voice was so near her ear, she felt the warmth of his breath on her cheek.

"These are known erosion holes into the Queen of Hearts." She tapped the marks she'd made courtesy of her conversation with Cheryl. "Those that are marked have been boarded over."

"And the ones that aren't marked?"

She didn't answer and he swore beneath his breath. She could only silently concur. There wasn't a soul living in these parts of Montana who wouldn't be familiar with the "Stay Out, Stay Alive" motto when it came to abandoned mines. It was taught in school, splashed across early Sunday morning public service announcements on television and painted on bus-stop benches.

All of which might mean absolutely nothing to an adventurous, curious young boy.

She folded the map and he handed her the penlight, which she pocketed. Then she started the snowmobile again and drove slowly along Miss Emelda's property line, her powerful searchlight steady thanks to Cameron's guidance. The entrance proper to the Queen of Hearts was a good two miles away. But the tunnels were surprisingly extensive, according to Cheryl, who had a grandfather several generations back who'd worked the Douglas-owned mine.

She nearly drove right over the first hole since the planks covering it were almost obscured by snow. Cameron swung off the cat and dropped to his knees, tunneling his hands through the snow to yank at the planks. They budged even less than Miss Emelda's garage doors had.

The wind skidded over them, lifting the dark hair on his unprotected head as he strode back to the snowmobile and climbed on behind her.

Did Erik's parka have a hood?

The snowmobile jumped forward, her anxiety unfortunately finding its way to the throttle, and Cameron's hands abruptly closed over her hips as he steadied himself. Ignoring him was impossible, but at least the sudden heat streaking through her helped hold the cold at bay. "What does Erik know about the mine?" She raised her voice so he could hear.

The entire length of her back felt the press of him as he leaned over her shoulder. "Nothing beyond what Emelda Ross talks about at the library."

If Miss Emelda were spinning her tales as enticingly now as she had when Faith was a child, she could only imagine the effect on an impressionable, adventurous boy. "Does he ever talk about it?"

"No."

Well. Okay. No wiggle room there.

She found the second site. Long, narrow and securely boarded over, though the board looked as if it had taken its share of potshots from a pellet gun or two.

The third site was also a bust.

Discouraged, Faith pulled out her map again. The sun was finally peeking over the horizon, but as it often did at dawn, the temperature seemed to drop several degrees in the process. There was also a low-lying layer of gray cloud that practically screamed *snow.* And she was glad for the solid warmth of the man behind her. "We had to have missed one." She studied the map. Turned and studied the physical landmarks around them.

"There." Cam reached around her and pointed at the map. "That would be, what? About fifty yards north."

He was right. She traced her gaze in that direction. There was an ebb and flow of snowdrifts along the fence line, in some places completely obscuring the wood rails. It was anybody's guess whose property it was. She figured they'd long passed Emelda Ross's land, which meant it was probably Douglas property, as was most of the open land.

The back of her neck prickled and she quickly folded the map. "Call for him." Her voice was practically hoarse from all the calling she had done.

The man needed no second urging. His deep voice boomed out as she maneuvered the cat around once more. Up, over the hills, fairly flying across the little valleys. And then she spotted the haphazard point of upended planks poking out of the snow.

Snow spewed from beneath the runners when she pulled to a stop nearby. Cam was off the cat before she could even form a warning to be cautious. He went flat on his stomach, his head disappearing below a jagged, splintered board that stuck up from the snow like some ancient spear. "Erik!"

Faith's knees went weak when they both heard the faint response.

At last. Thank you, God.

They'd found him.

Chapter Three

"*Erik!*" Cam stared into the dark pit. His eyes burned. "Are you hurt?" He could hear his son's muffled sobs. His fingers tightened on the board, oblivious to the dagger-sharp splinters that tore through his gloves. "We're gonna get you out in a sec," he promised roughly.

He looked back to see Faith speaking into her radio even as she dragged equipment out of the cargo beneath the seat of the snowmobile. Rope. Harness. Shovel.

She ran over to him, surprisingly adept even though her legs sunk into the snow nearly to her knees with each step, and dumped the items beside him. "I need to see down there." She waited until he'd moved back and she leaned carefully over the narrow opening, peering down. "Erik, I'm going to throw down some light sticks, okay?"

His answer was too long in coming. But eventually, his young voice floated upward. "'Kay."

She quickly shook a few sticks—pulled from one of her many pockets—to activate them and tossed them down. "Fire's sending a truck," she said without looking back at Cam. "My boss, Jim, is going to try to get here, but it's gonna take at least an hour before he can get a chopper free. We need to get some of this snow cleared." She grabbed the shovel and began attacking the white weight.

Cam helped, scooping away snow with his hands, then his arm, until they could see the full scope of the boarded-over hole.

Nausea curled its nasty fingers into him.

Faith sat back, the short shovel resting on her thighs. "He was looking down where those boards are pulled away, and this one gave way beneath him." They both eyed the freshly split plank.

There'd only been four planks to start with. About eight feet long, covering the opening that was—at best—half that long and even less than that wide. Only one board remained intact, but when she tested its solidity, dirt and snow rained down into the crevice.

"Daddy!" Erik's voice howled up.

"It's okay, Erik," he yelled down. Then he eyed Faith. "I'm not waiting."

"Yes, you are." She caught him in a surprisingly

strong grip when he reached for the rope. "Your son didn't climb down there. He fell. We're going to need help to get him out."

He shrugged her off. "I am *not* waiting." He stood up, grabbing the rope, eyeing the best place to tie it off. The old snow fence with boards as ruinous as what was supposed to have protected the erosion hole, or the snowmobile that was massive only if he compared it to Faith Taylor's size rather than his own? "He's down there, crying, and there's no way a fire crew can get across that snow."

The sunlight was even stronger now—he saw the flicker in her hazel eyes and knew she'd thought the same thing. They'd been able to traverse the deep snow only because of the snowmobile. If a fire crew were to make it to them, they'd either need to be following a snowplow, have a fleet of snowmobiles—which they didn't exactly have considering half of it had already been used by Faith—or be on foot with cross-country skies or snowshoes.

"There's no way you can even *fit*," she countered, her voice flat as she eyed his shoulders.

"Daddy!" Erik's wail was faint. "Iwannagetoutta heeeere!"

Ignoring Faith, Cam headed toward the snowmobile. As an anchor, it was the best they had. He cinched the rope around it, and started carrying the rest of the coiled rope back toward the hole, only to be sideswiped by a hundred and twenty pounds of irate female.

The snow cushioned their fall but the impact still

knocked him for six. He stared up at the sky, at the blonde nearly sitting on his chest. "What the hell are you doing?"

"Maybe football tackles are the only thing you understand." Her voice was tight and her eyes flashed. "I am *not* letting you endanger yourself, too."

He lifted her bodily from him and dumped her on her backside. "And you obviously don't know what it's like to have a child in danger."

The high color in her cheeks drained right back out. "That doesn't mean I don't care about the child who *is*," she said stiffly. "For your son's sake, let me do my job!"

"What? *You're* going to go down there?"

She pushed to her feet and stomped through the deep snow back to the snowmobile, where she began untying his knot.

"Faith, dammit—"

She shot him a killing glare and he realized she was tying a fresh one. "At least learn how to tie a knot that won't slip." Her voice was cutting. "I may be the only female SAR in this county, Mr. Stevenson, but I've earned my place on this team." She shouldered the rest of the coiled rope and kicked her way through the snow past him toward the hole. "Do you know how many times we end up having to get *two* people out of difficulties because someone was foolhardy enough to enter a situation they weren't prepared or qualified for because they were so intent on solving the problem themselves?" As she spoke, she was working the rope through the harness and a series of pulleys. "Too many. Frankly—" she shot him a dark look "—I have better things to do with my time than rescue a father whose concern for his son comes a little late."

"What the hell is *that* supposed to mean?"

Faith shook her head and carefully stepped over the one remaining undamaged board, ignoring Cameron's furious voice. Looking down, she could see the faint, green glow of the light sticks. She was going down because she couldn't stand to listen to Erik's woeful cries a moment longer, and for no other reason. "I'm coming down there, Erik," she called loudly.

And when Jim showed up and found out she'd acted without backup, she'd probably lose her hard-won spot on the SAR team.

She stepped off the board, and the rope whizzed as she descended into the narrow crevice. The farther she went, the more obvious it became that Cameron— even if he'd tried—would never have managed to fit. Not when it was so close around her.

"Erik?" She braced her legs against the dirt walls on either side of her, and slowly began maneuvering out of her coat. "My name is Faith Taylor. How ya' doing down there?"

"I'm cold."

She was sweating. And his voice was definitely weak. "I'll bet you are." She finally worked out of the sleeves and simply let the thing fall. She needed the extra few inches of space she'd gain without it. "My coat is coming down. If you can grab it, go ahead. Did you hurt anything when you fell?"

"I dunno." His crying abated a little. "Oh. There goes your coat. I, um, I missed it."

"That's okay. It's just a coat." She lowered a few more inches, carefully working her shoulders past an embedded rock that had already painfully caught her hip. "Did you hit your head when you fell?"

"I think so. It hurts a lot. Where's my dad?"

"He's waiting for you up top," she assured gently as she worked a little faster. His words were slurring. Concussion? Exposure? Both?

Regardless, she wanted to keep him talking and alert. "Erik, are you on a ledge or something?"

"'S wood. I got splinters in my bu—rear."

And she was mighty grateful he was in fair enough shape to sound indignant about it. "What were you doing all the way out here?"

"Dad's gonna ground me for a year."

"Maybe." Her voice was cheerful, masking her tension. "My parents grounded me once for six months." She finally cleared the rock, only to duck her head when a cascade of dirt rained down on her. When it stopped, she looked up. She could see Cameron leaning over the hole. "Don't suppose Fire is here yet?" she called up to him.

"No."

And Jim obviously wasn't, either, or he'd be haranguing her.

"What'd they ground ya' for?"

Faith slid down another foot. She figured she was about thirty feet down. "I went climbing in the canyon without permission. And I ended up breaking my arm.

And since nobody knew where I was...well, once they found me and had finished hugging me, they grounded me."

Erik had no reply to that. He might only be seven, but she hoped he was grasping her point and not falling unconscious. "Erik? You still with me?"

"Uh-huh."

The hole widened again and she tugged a flashlight out of the cargo pocket on her calf. She flipped it on, shining it around, then down. She could see Erik's feet another fifteen feet or so below her and she lowered herself the rest of the way.

Her flashlight danced over him, catching his dirt-smudged face. She caught her toes over the wood beam and steadied herself. "Hey there. Think you can hold my light?"

"Yeah."

She reached out, handing the light to him. "Shine it downward, though. Okay?"

The beam redirected away from her eyes.

"Kinda scary down here, huh?"

"I think there might be bats or something."

Faith doubted it, but she wanted to keep the boy talking. The rough beam was incredibly unstable and she didn't dare use it to take her weight. Only problem was, she couldn't ascend with him, because there wasn't enough space, and she couldn't rig her second harness around him unless she had a steady foothold. Which meant she'd have to take him down lower with her, before she could get him up.

"You're a girl."

She grinned. "'Fraid so. Only seven-year-olds and girls could fit down that hole up there. Think you can scoot closer to me, Erik?"

He started to, but the wood moaned and debris tumbled loose. She held up her hand. "Okay. So that's not gonna work."

"I want my dad," he whispered.

Her heart squeezed. "I know you do, sweetie. Here's the deal. I'm going to swing over closer to you in a minute, and you're gonna grab onto me good and tight, then we'll lower down into the mine shaft below us, okay?"

"I don't wanna go down *more!*" Panic riddled his words.

"Believe me, you've come down the worst of it, already," she assured calmly. "I just need to know if you can grab onto me. Really fast. I'll catch you, too, at the same time."

"What if I fall?"

"I won't let you."

"But—"

"Erik? The quicker we do this, the quicker I can get you up top again. Or we can wait until one of my friends gets here." Not that Jim would fit down the hole any easier than Cameron would have.

"How long's that gonna take?"

"I don't know, sweetie. Might be an hour or so."

"I gotta pee," he whispered. "And my head hurts really, really bad."

Her throat tightened. "I can't do anything about your head just yet, but you could go down here. I won't tell anyone."

"Dad said I'm not s'posed to do that 'cause it's bad manners, just like I'm not s'posed to call grown-ups by their first name."

She bit back a smile at the odd pairing of rules. "Ordinarily I'd agree," she murmured. "But I think this would be considered extenuating circumstances. I'll turn my back. Give you some privacy. And you can call me Faith. It's okay, when you've gotten permission from an adult."

He looked torn. "I'll jus' catch you."

"All rightee then." She reached forward and took the flashlight back and returned it to her calf pocket. "I don't want you to move your legs or anything. Just reach out with your arms." She was too afraid of the beam toppling if he did more than that. "When I count to three, you be ready, okay?"

"'Kay." His voice was breathless. She hoped it was only from formulating the stories he'd be able to share after this was all over.

"One." She adjusted her grip on the rope, prepared to pull up or let down depending on what the beam did. "Two." She pressed the toe of her boot against the wall of dirt for leverage. "Three."

She swung toward him and a set of young arms grabbed onto her like a lifeline and she scooped him up, taking on his fifty pounds as the rope whizzed and they descended into the mineshaft.

Her feet hit solid ground with a jolt and she carefully knelt, settling him on the earth. "I don't want you to move, okay? Just in case you *have* hurt something you don't know about." She waited until he focused on her, then stood and unhooked the second harness from her belt.

She walked a few feet until she could see daylight at the top of the hole. "I've got him," she called up. "He'll be coming up in a few minutes."

She saw Cameron's arm lift. The man was probably too choked up to speak. Her conscience bit at her some for speaking so harshly to him, but she ignored it and turned her focus back to Erik.

"So." She tugged off her gloves and pulled out her flashlight again to shine it over him as she crouched next to him. "Seriously. What *were* you doing coming out here by yourself?"

"Wasn't by myself," he defended. "I was with Tommy Bodecker, 'cause it was his dare."

Good Lord. Save her from boyhood dares. She slowly felt along his arms and legs. "Is Tommy in your class at school?"

"Nah. He's ten already."

"And where's Tommy now?" She wasn't familiar with the Bodecker family.

Erik made a face. "He went home 'cause it started to snow."

"I see. And you didn't go with him, because… *why?*"

"'Cause of the dare," he said as if it should be perfectly obvious. "He said I was ascared of ghosts an' I told him I was not. And he said if I wasn't then how come I never came out here and saw 'em for myself."

"Ghosts. I see. Tommy Bodecker thinks there are ghosts here in the mine?"

"Yeah." Erik flinched a little when she ran her fingers over his shoulder, but he didn't complain.

"So when he left you out here by yourself, you figured you had to stay." She discovered the enormous goose egg behind his ear. "And prove you weren't scared."

His expression was approving. "Yeah."

She'd have a few things to say to Tommy Bodecker if and when she caught up to him. "I think I might have heard of it if Tommy had ever spent the night in the Queen of Hearts," she murmured. "So if anyone's the authority on ghosts here, that'd be you."

"Oh." A dimple snuck out from his cheeks. "Yeah."

"So? Were there any ghosts?"

He shook his head.

"Just bats?"

He nodded.

He was adorable. "Think you can stand up so I can get you into this harness?"

He scrambled to his feet, hunching over a little, definitely off balance. She steadied him as she helped him into the rescue harness, adjusting the webbing, fastening off her rope to him.

"What do I gotta do?"

"Not a thing," she promised. "I've got you roped off up top. I'm just going to pull on this end, and you're going to lift out. Simple as can be." She suited actions to words and his feet left the ground.

"Cool."

"It's cool that I can get you out of here," she said, bringing him eye-level with her. "If you want to learn how to climb, you should do it properly next time. Ever seen the rock climbing gym at Extension Sporting Goods?"

His eyes were enormous. "I seen it, but my dad's never let me do it."

"Tell him they give classes there. You ready to go?"

He nodded.

"Just tell me if you want me to slow you down or anything. If you feel sick to your stomach or anything."

His head bobbed yet again and he winced, going still. "I hurt."

She gently ran her hand over his tousled hair. "I know, sweetie. But you're going to be okay."

"Dad's mad."

"He's gladder that we found you," she promised. "Ready?"

His eyelashes were drooping. "Uh-huh."

She began working the rope, levering him upward. It took less time to raise him to the top than it had for her to make the descent. And she knew the moment he was close enough for Cameron to grab hold, because the weight of him was immediately lifted from her braced body. Moments later, the rope snaked back down to her again.

She let out a long breath and willed her legs to stop shaking. She could hear the high pitch of Erik's voice and the lower murmur of Cameron's and didn't have to work hard to imagine the relief that would be in the man's deep brown eyes.

Pulling out her flashlight again, she played its light

over her confines. In both directions, the tunnel had completely caved in. Directly above her was none too stable, either, considering the rotting timber on which Erik had managed to land.

It was considerably warmer below surface, though, which was a blessing. If Erik had been more exposed during the storm—

She cut off the thought. Her coat lay in a shadowy heap and she grabbed it, tying it off her belt. Her hip ached with a sharp throb where she'd connected with the embedded rock. She could only imagine the bumps Erik had sustained.

She moved until she could see sky again. "Use the radio," she called up. "Find out what's holding them up. Erik needs medical attention."

Cameron's head appeared. "Already called. Ambulance is on its way," he yelled back.

Well. She had to give the man credit for thinking.

And now that Erik was up top, the effects of the last day were definitely starting to wear on her. She wanted a hot bath and sleep.

Neither of which she was going to get if she didn't get herself out of the mine.

If the ambulance or Fire hadn't managed to make their way to them by the time Faith made it out, she'd tell Cam to take Erik to the hospital on the snowmobile. They could always send someone back for her.

In this section of the mine shaft, there was no wall to climb up, and the rotting beams that had caught Erik were too unstable to use as support. So she climbed the rope. Hand over hand, rope snaking between her twisted boots. For the first time in a long while, she actually felt grateful for the number of times her ex-husband had challenged her on the ropes while they'd been living in Albuquerque.

"How are you coming?"

Cameron's voice startled her and she jerked a little, knocking her knee on one of the beams. The wood creaked and debris fell. "Coming up," she told him, carefully pulling herself up the thick rope, beyond the treacherous wood. She was starting to feel light-headed and wasn't certain if it was simply hunger, the expulsion of her adrenaline, or the air quality in the mine. Whatever it was, it made her stop for a moment, suspended there on the rope, as she waited for the spinning to stop.

A lovely time to remember that neither rock climbing nor ropes had ever been her favorite pastime.

At last, she heard the whine of a siren coming closer.

She swallowed, and cautiously began again. But when she reached that same, particularly narrow patch with the rock her hip had already greeted intimately, she had to slow again.

Even though she'd tied the coat off and it hung harmlessly down behind her, it still created too much bulk. She pulled it loose and let it fall again. Pity. They had to buy their own uniforms and those coats didn't come cheap. Her sweatshirt wasn't much of a help, either, she discovered, and she inched down a bit on the rope, twining her legs tightly to keep her balance, and worked out of it, leaving her with only the thin waffle-weave of her thermal undershirt. But it gave her the quarter-inch she needed, and she started to squeeze past the obstruction, earning herself a fresh set of scrapes and bruises in the process.

But just when she thought she was within sight of passing it, another cascade of dirt rained down on her head, blinding her. She swore, ducking, and lost several precious inches. The dirt just kept coming, piling in around her, filling in the bare spaces between her body and the eroding walls.

Panic nipped at her with nasty teeth. The downfall eased and she finally lifted her head, squinting against the dust that wanted to attack her eyes.

"Cameron!" His name was a hoarse yell.

"I got you." His voice was audible, though she couldn't make him out beyond the swirling dirt. "The last board collapsed. Ground's caving in."

She wriggled, trying to turn her hipbone away from the rock. Something caught. A strap of her harness. A fold of her pants. Something. She coughed, spitting dirt out of her mouth. Freeing one hand to wipe at her face. "I'm stuck!"

She could hear him swearing. "I'm gonna pull you up."

The rope went tight as a wire. She could feel it dragging at her, as surely as she could feel the earth keeping her in its greedy grasp.

"Wait!" Tears burned her eyes. It felt like she was being split into two.

The rope eased. She tilted her head back. The hole up top was wider, yet it was filling up where she was pinned as if she were some thumb plugging up a dike. Cameron stared down at her. The siren was growing louder.

It felt as if hours had passed since she'd lifted the boy out of the mine, but she knew it was only minutes.

"Keep Erik away from the hole."

"He's sitting by the snowmobile."

There was still space for her feet to move. She felt around, seeking some leverage to push up, but found none. Her toes were getting numb and the pressure on her chest was making her dizzy. Her hand was trapped near her abdomen and she worked her fingers around until she found a buckle.

"What are you doing down there?"

"Having a tea party," she muttered. "I have to get out of my harness," she said as loudly as her compressed chest allowed.

"What do you need from me?"

"A shovel, if more dirt comes down here." She coughed. Every time she inhaled, she got a lungful of dust, and with her free hand, she stretched the collar of her thermal shirt up over her chin and nose.

"At least you've got a sense of humor," she heard him say.

At least he got the fact she'd been facetious.

Her fingers strained to work the webbed strap free. There was no question of when the buckle loosened, because she felt an immediate release of pressure pulling down on her hips. She held tightly to the rope with her free hand as she wriggled a little more, trying to gain more space. She could feel the warmth of blood where her skin was being torn away by the immovable rock. Her boots scrabbled and she finally managed to pull herself upward a few precious inches. She exhaled, sucked in her stomach, and scraped past the rock. At last, her other hand was free, and she grabbed the rope with it. "Okay, now pull." The siren was so loud now, she wasn't sure he'd even hear her.

Her voice was barely audible, but Cam heard. He braced himself and pulled on the rope. Not that she weighed much. But every time he moved his foot, he feared another cubic foot of earth was going to collapse in on her.

And he still had one eye on his son. Erik had lain on his side in the snow. "Erik!" His voice was rough.

His boy lifted his hand slightly, and relief eased the vise around his heart. But Faith was still hanging on to the end of the rope.

He dragged on it, hauling it upward. Faith's head appeared and he grabbed her shoulders, bodily lifting her the rest of the way just as the ambulance, preceded by a snowplow, arrived. Two police vehicles followed.

He pulled Faith clear of the crumbling hole, plunged several feet away and settled her in the snow. It seemed a better choice, rather than keeping her tightly against him. Her fingers were still locked around the rope and he carefully loosened them. Her knuckles were raw. Bloody. He'd tended plenty of banged up football players—broken noses, broken legs, split lips. The sight of blood had never bothered him before.

It did now. He didn't even have something clean and soft to wrap around her hands.

"See to Erik." Her voice was husky. She was caked with dirt, but he could still see the blood seeping through her skinny white thermal shirt. More blood.

"Can you walk?" He tore out of his coat and cautiously pulled it around her shoulders, shaking off the unwelcome urge to wrap his arms around her as well.

"I'm okay." The fuzziness in her hazel eyes was already starting to clear. She turned her head, looking back at the erosion hole. "Thank you."

Cam shoved his shaking hand through his hair. "Thank *you*," he said huskily. Then, because he couldn't leave her lying in the snow any more than he could leave his son for a moment longer, he scooped her up.

"I can walk," she muttered. But her head still fell tiredly to his shoulder. Ignoring her protest, he carried her over to where the paramedic was bending over Erik.

"She's bleeding," he announced, settling her on the seat of the snowmobile. Letting go was harder than it should have been, and he took a few steps away. As if he could step away from the knot she caused inside him.

The paramedic lifted his blond head and Cam realized the man wasn't a paramedic at all, but one of the doctors from the hospital.

"What're you doing here?" Faith asked the man.

"You kidding? The whole town's talking about you finding Erik down in the Queen of Hearts."

Faith's lips twisted a little. Her gaze flicked up to Cameron. "This is my brother. Dr. Christopher Taylor." Then she looked back at Erik, who was staring at her as if she'd sprouted wings. "How's he doing?"

"Good, considering." The doctor grinned at Cam's son, and the resemblance between the Taylors became even more apparent. "I want to run some tests, check him in for observation for a few days, just to be safe."

"I don't wanna."

"You hit your head pretty hard, pal," the doctor said smoothly. "We need to make sure you heal up okay from that."

"Daddy?"

Cam crouched down beside Erik. His hands shook as he smoothed back his son's hair. His boy had his coloring, but every time he looked at Erik, he saw so much of Laura looking back at him. How would he have gone on if he'd lost Erik, too? "I'll go with you."

The ambulance driver and the snowplow driver stood by with a stretcher, and the doctor placed Erik on it. He'd already hooked up an IV to Erik's arm and he handed the bag to Cam to carry alongside. "For dehydration," he said.

They started for the ambulance, but Cam hesitated. "What about Faith?"

She waved her hand. "Go. I'll be fine."

The doctor snorted. "Hardly. You're going, too, Faith."

She lifted an eyebrow, clearly rallying. "Not today, Topher."

Judging by the tone in her voice, the nickname

wasn't one the doctor particularly enjoyed hearing. And the man obviously wanted to argue. But there was no hiding his urgency in getting Erik to the hospital. Cam was feeling pretty urgent, too.

"Go." Faith waved her hand. "I can bandage up my own scrapes."

The doctor leaned over and whipped Faith's shirt up above her waist. Cam winced even as Faith was jerking her shirt back down over the torn pants and raw flesh. "You need to go to the hospital," he said flatly. "And not on that snowmobile."

"I'll go by after I've had a shower," she said stiffly. "And I *won't* take the snowmobile."

"If you don't, Faith—" Doctor Taylor cut off his threat when Erik wretched.

"Go," Faith insisted to Cam as the doc tended his son. "There's not room in the ambulance for all of us. I'll grab a ride with the uniforms." She waved a hand toward the police officers who were struggling through the snow toward the dangerous hole. "I'll send someone back later for the cat. And Cam's truck."

Then, as if the matter was settled, Faith leaned over, grabbed her radio, and began speaking into it. She hardly seemed to notice her injured fingers.

The doctor quickly loaded Erik into the ambulance and Cam moved aside in the confined space to make room for Dr. Taylor. In seconds, the ambulance lurched and began crunching over the frozen ground.

Through the rear window, Cam watched Faith Taylor. She looked incredibly small inside the bulk of his coat.

If she hadn't gone down to get his son when she had, Erik might have still been down there when the hole caved in even more.

"Remarkable, isn't she?" Dr. Taylor's voice was quiet.

Cam dragged his gaze away from the woman. His fingers tightened around Erik's small hand. "Remarkable," he agreed after a moment.

And he owed his son's safety to her.

But that still didn't mean he welcomed the effect she had on him.

Chapter Four

The only thing holding Faith upright was the door-jamb of her front door against her spine. She waved at Teddy as he departed. She'd ended up riding back with the snowplow driver since it had quickly become clear that the police would be occupied for a while securing the erosion hole.

As soon as the snowplow lumbered down the street, however, she slunk inside her condo and nudged the door closed. Cameron Stevenson's coat slid off her shoulders and she left it where it lay, shuffling straight to the bathroom.

She flipped on the shower, letting the room fill with steam while she summoned enough stamina to peel out of her clothes. When she did, a cloud of dirt puffed out to settle on the pale green rug. She ignored that, too, and stepped under the hot spray, wincing as the water found her wounds and swirled around her feet in a cloud of dirt and blood. She rinsed the worst of the dirt from her hair and the moment she felt reasonably clean, she flipped the rush of water from the showerhead to the faucet, and filled the tub, sinking down with relief.

She soaked until her skin pruned and the water cooled. And then, because her muscles were stiffening beyond belief, she made herself get out of the tub before it got any worse. She gingerly spread antibiotic ointment over her cuts and scrapes, used up every bandage she managed to unearth in her medicine cabinet, then padded barefoot into her bedroom.

She was so tired she could barely keep her eyes open. She opened her closet and pulled a clean oversize T-shirt from a neat stack. As she did so, her gaze lifted, as it always did, to the pastel items folded on the top shelf.

Then she firmly closed the door and climbed into bed, pulling her quilt up to her ears. The phone rang, but she ignored it, knowing her answering machine would pick it up eventually.

Once she'd had a nap, she'd go check on Erik at the hospital.

But it wasn't the boy who was on her mind when she fell asleep moments later.

It was the boy's father.

"Pull a stunt like that again, Taylor, and you're off the team." Jim Shepherd's eyes were level as he stood smack-dab in the corridor outside Thunder Canyon General's pediatric unit. Faith hadn't managed to visit Erik at the hospital the prior day, simply because she'd slept clean through to the next morning. Now, after spending the morning at the fire station, it was lunchtime, and she simply was not going to be delayed any longer.

Not even by her boss, who'd been dogging her heels for ten minutes. He also hadn't made it to Thunder Canyon the previous day. But he was making up for not getting to the site of Erik's accident now by raking her over the coals.

"I'm serious, Faith. We don't enter abandoned mines without backup."

She didn't mind the raking when she'd earned it. But she couldn't—wouldn't—change the decision she'd made. "Well, as I've said about a dozen times now, the only backup I had handy was Cameron Stevenson. It would have taken a demo crew to get through to Erik from the mine shaft itself. Any access points had already collapsed."

"But you didn't know that beforehand, did you?"

She couldn't deny that point, so she just stood there, eyeing her boss.

After a moment, he sighed noisily, then looked around the hospital, with its pale walls and stark tile floors.

"*The Nugget* wants an interview about the rescue."

"Give 'em one if you want." Faith had already erased the message from the local reporter who'd called the previous day. "I don't have anything to say."

Jim wasn't particularly enamored with the publicity their team often garnered, but he was also aware of the fact that their salaries came from the same people who read those newspapers. "Evidently, during the cleanup, somebody found a small gold nugget."

Faith shrugged. "I didn't notice any gold," she said dryly. "I was a little busy."

He smiled a little. "So how's the kid?"

"Concussion. Dehydration." The answer didn't come from Faith, and she stiffened, looking past Jim to see Cameron standing there.

Her gaze roved over him before she could stop herself. The handsome man with the broad shoulders had hauled her out of a very sticky situation, she silently defended. Of course she had some…enhanced interest in him. It was gratitude.

Which didn't at all explain the odd curling sensation inside her stomach. Or the reason his coat was still laying on the couch in her living room like some welcome visitor.

His brown gaze was steady on her face and she was positively mortified to feel her cheeks warming. "Jim, this is Cameron Stevenson," she introduced hurriedly. Anything to restore normalcy. "Mr. Stevenson, this is Jim Shepherd, my boss."

The two men shook hands. "Glad things worked out okay," Jim said. He was probably ten years older than the mid-thirties in which she'd privately placed Cameron. Jim also was not as tall, nor as broad.

And comparing her boss to Cameron's wealth of physical attributes seemed a ridiculous waste of time.

"How is Erik today? I meant to get over here yesterday."

"He's terrorizing the nurses," he said. "He's been asking after you."

Her spurt of pleasure at that news dwindled quickly when Faith felt Jim's gaze silently travel from Cameron to her and back again. She wished she didn't know what the man was thinking. He'd been happily married for twenty years, and in the year since she'd been on the team, he'd made no secret that he figured she needed a man in her life again. Judging by his speculative expression, she could only imagine where his thoughts were going now.

"I hope you've made time to get yourself treated, too," Cameron said. "Since you didn't do it yesterday."

The palm of her hand snuck across her hip where several large gauze pads lurked beneath her clothing, and the way his sharp brown gaze veered down for a fraction of a moment told her that her self-conscious movement hadn't gone unnoticed. "How'd you know I didn't come in?"

"Dr. Taylor mentioned it."

"Treated?" Jim didn't look pleased. "You were injured? That wasn't in your report."

"A few bumps," Faith defended evenly. "Nothing that necessitates my brother's overdeveloped sense of protection."

"But since you're here at the hospital, you might as well let him take a look at you." Cameron's voice was smoothly reasonable. "You were bleeding a lot when you came out of the mine."

"You want me to put you on inactive?" Jim asked, knowing full well that she'd go bananas without work to occupy her time.

She really did not like feeling ganged up on. But how could she tell them just how much she loathed going to a doctor, any doctor, even for something as minor as patching up her scrapes? "I'll go after I've seen Erik." She mentally crossed her fingers. "Is he awake?"

In answer, Cameron pushed open the door to his son's private room. Faith hesitated for a moment, then stepped past him. And she did *not* notice how good he smelled, either.

She focused on the boy, who seemed to be nearly swallowed by the hospital bed, though she figured Erik was pretty average-size for his age. "Hey there, kiddo."

"Faith! You came."

Warmth filled her at the way Erik's expression lit. She put Erik's dad out of her mind as far as he would go—admittedly not very far, if she were honest—as she approached the bed and handed Erik the large box that was wrapped in bright blue paper patterned with footballs, basketballs and baseballs. "You can't use it until your doctor gives you the say-so, though," she warned when his hands grabbed onto the gift.

"Can I open it now?" There was such hope in his sparkling brown eyes that if he hadn't already charmed her, he would have done so now.

She laughed softly. "That's sort of the point," she assured. "Open away."

"Yessss." His fingers dragged at the wrapping, and paper flew. Then his jaw dropped a little, his eyes widening, when the neon green soft toboggan was revealed. "Kew-ell," he dragged out the word. "I always wanted one of these, but Dad wouldn't let me."

She felt a stab of guilt at that, wondering if she should have asked permission from Cameron before giving the gift to Erik. She had no nieces or nephews. Was there some sort of etiquette she should have known to follow?

On the table beside the bed were a stack of video games, and she had a qualm that she ought to have brought something similar. And judging by Cameron's expression, he wasn't all that pleased with the gift.

But all he said was, "What do you say, Erik?"

Erik looked chagrined. "Right. Thank you, Faith."

"Ms. Taylor," Cameron prompted.

"Uh-uh," Erik countered. "She told me I could call her Faith. Right?"

She nodded. "Yes, I did. When are they going to spring you?"

Erik rolled his eyes. "I just wanna leave now."

Behind Cameron, Jim lifted his hand in a wave, gesturing with his pager, before heading off. Cameron walked into the room, letting the door swish closed. "They told us he'll be ready to go home by Wednesday."

"Maybe Faith can come over and show me how to use the toboggan, huh, Dad?"

He didn't approach the bed where Faith was standing, she noticed, but remained closer to the door. Almost as if he couldn't wait to open it again and have her leave.

"I'd love to," she told the boy, though it seemed unfathomable to her that any child living in Thunder Canyon hadn't already had *some* experience with tobogganing. There was a hill near the ice-skating rink that was perfect for sledding and snowboarding, and during snow season, it was nearly always congested with children.

"We'll see," Cameron said.

Faith eyed him for a moment, but being well aware of Erik's avid attention, she held her tongue. Instead, she grinned at the boy. "Any word from Tommy Bodecker about ghosts?"

Erik started to speak, but Cameron was the one who answered. "Erik won't be hanging out with Tommy anymore." His voice was flat.

Faith could hardly blame the man for that. She resisted the urge to smooth the cowlick on Erik's forehead. "Guess maybe he won't be issuing dares anymore, eh?"

He started to smile, but it died as he shot his dad a wary look. "No, ma'am."

Ma'am. Ouch. "Well, you just let me know when you're up to trying out this puppy." She tapped the colorful sled. "And I'm glad you'll be getting out of here soon."

"Thanks." Erik's smile was ever so much easier than his father's.

She winked at the boy, and headed to the door. Her steps slowed, though, as she waited for Cameron to move out of the way, and when he followed her into the hall once more, she hoped the jumping in her stomach wasn't visible on her face.

"Did you get your truck back okay from Miss Emelda's place?"

He nodded once.

She brushed her palms down her thighs. "I, um, I hope you don't mind. You know. About the gift for Erik."

"It was nice of you to think of him."

"He's had other visitors?" She certainly hoped so. She could only imagine how tedious it would be if he didn't have some entertainment.

"A few of his school friends have come by. Adele Douglas came by yesterday, too. Said she wanted to see for her own eyes that he was going to be fine." It was Adele and Caleb Douglas who owned the mine.

Faith listened with half an ear. She noticed that Cameron didn't move out of the doorway to Erik's room. He was obviously keeping an eye on his son, inside.

"He's not going to disappear from the hospital room," she said softly. Did he think the boy was going to dash out the window and try out the unwelcome toboggan?

"First you think I don't watch him closely enough, and now you think I watch him too closely?" His voice was audible only to her ears.

Since his assessment was fairly accurate, she wasn't sure how to respond. And then there was the bungee jumping her stomach was doing. A decidedly unfamiliar sensation, but not one that she couldn't pinpoint to a very specific source—namely one six-foot-plus man. "It's none of my business," she finally settled on, which was also true enough.

Some of the lines had left his face, and his square jaw was again smooth-shaven and far too masculine and appealing.

She shifted, pushing her hands in the front pockets of her khakis. Learning that her libido was evidently alive and well wasn't necessarily a particularly welcome thing. "I, um, really should be going." She'd told Tanya that she'd help out at the sporting goods store that afternoon. "I'd like to come by and see Erik again." When he didn't tell her to stay away, she took it as a good sign. Nodding again, feeling awkward and not liking it one bit, she turned to go.

"The Bodeckers came by and apologized." His voice forestalled her. "Apparently, they didn't realize Tommy was missing at all from the reception, because he was back at The Hall before they even left."

She halted and looked back. It had to be her imagination that he was deliberately delaying her departure. "And when word got out that Erik was missing? Why didn't Tommy speak up *then?*"

Cam shook his head, keeping his fists from curling. But it took an effort. Just as it took an effort not to stare at her face—so female, so golden—as she looked up at him. "Evidently, he'd been grounded for a few weeks. No television. No radio. When his folks went to the wedding, they dragged him along with him." Same as he'd dragged Erik.

"Well." Faith's eyes didn't meet his. "This is one of those times to concentrate on the fact that everything turned out all right."

He made a noncommittal noise and then her gaze did lift to his, and it felt as if the collision jolted the ground right under him.

Dammit.

"*Is* it all right?" She lowered her voice even more. "If Erik's so fine, why does he have to stay two more days in the hospital?"

"Precaution. He had a pretty good concussion going."

Her lips pressed softly together. "But he'll be fine?"

How many times had Cam, himself, fired that question at Erik's doctor? He nodded, and there was no denying the relief that softened those brownish-green eyes of hers.

"Well, for once the rumor mill of Thunder Canyon General is on the mark. Heard you'd stepped foot on our holy grounds."

Faith's expression tightened a little as she turned to see her brother striding in their direction.

"Don't you have duties in the E.R.?" she asked pointedly.

Dr. Taylor grinned, but his blue eyes, when he glanced at Cam, were serious. "More patients than Carter's got pills," he agreed. "Your boss stopped by. Heard you're going on inactive until we give you a medical clearance."

"I came to see Erik, not get poked at by a sadist in a white lab coat."

"Hey. I resent that remark."

Judging by her expression, Cam figured she wasn't amused. "Chris—"

"Just a once-over," the doctor interrupted. "We've got a new crop of residents. You can take your pick of 'em."

The look she sent her brother was killing. "Fine." She nodded at Cam and strode off down the hall.

Realizing the doctor was watching him, Cam dragged his attention away from the impeccable fit of Faith's khaki pants. There was an unholy gleam in Christopher Taylor's eyes now, though, that told Cam the other man knew exactly what Cam had been eyeing.

And why.

"Town's buzzing about Friday's game," was all the other man said. "People wanting to know when you're gonna put Romance back on the court."

"When he's not failing every class but PE," Cam said evenly. He'd taken plenty of heat about the decision to bench the boy.

The younger man just nodded, though. "Fair decision. You've got eyes for my sister?"

He figured it was his own preoccupation over Erik's safety that Cam hadn't seen that one coming. "She saved my son's life," he hedged.

"Mmm. True enough." The doctor suddenly reached for his hip and the pager that hung on the waist of his scrubs. "Duty calls." He lifted his hand and waved at Erik inside the room, then strode away.

Cam wasn't sure quite what to make of either one of the blond Taylors.

He went back into Erik's room, resigned to an afternoon of his son's chatter about his favorite new toy…Faith Taylor.

Faith winced when the resident—a young guy who looked as if he were all of twelve years old—finished cleaning the worst of her cuts and spread antibiotic ointment over them, followed by fresh gauze pads.

The rattle of the blue-and-white striped curtain partitioning off the bed from the others in the E.R. gave her little warning before her brother appeared. She gave him a baleful look as he eyed the bandages covering most of her hip and nearly all of her abdomen, and deliberately pulled her shirt down before zipping up her loosened pants.

Chris, with his typical equanimity, ignored her and simply took the chart from the child-doctor, glancing over it. He scribbled his pen across it after a moment, and handed back the chart.

"Go," he said humorously, when the boy still hovered there.

The resident went.

Chris rolled his eyes. "Seems like they're getting younger every year," he murmured.

"Only because you're getting *older*," Faith pointed out a trifle wickedly. At thirty-two, Chris was the eldest of the four Taylor children.

Chris merely lifted an eyebrow. "Someone looking thirty in the face ought to know enough to respect her elders," he pointed out. "So what's the deal with the Stevenson duo?"

Faith frowned and slid off the examining table. "Nothing."

"Right. *Nothing* got you past the cafeteria in this place."

"I just wanted to make sure he was doing all right." She fussed with the sleeves of her cotton shirt, folding them up her arms, then back down again.

"Which *he?*"

"Erik, of course." She hoped her cheeks weren't as fiery looking as they felt. "He's a cute boy. How, um, how long have they been in Thunder Canyon? Do you know?"

"Since the kid was an infant, I think." He thought about it a moment. "Cam didn't start teaching at the high school until after his wife died, though. He was some sort of financial whiz from Denver."

"I didn't ask for details."

"No. But you wanted to."

Faith snorted softly. "You're into reading minds now?"

"It's a big brother thing," he assured blandly. "If you'd come in yesterday when I wanted you to, we could have stitched up the worst of those cuts of yours. You'll probably have a helluva scar."

"It won't be the first one," she muttered. She had an assortment of old, fading scars on her elbows, her knees. All courtesy of never quite being the girly-girl daughter her mother had wanted. Fortunately, her two younger sisters, Hope and Jill, had been more than feminine enough to make up for Faith's failings.

They'd be the ones to provide the next generation

of Taylors, too. Unless Chris ever got off his duff and got serious about a woman himself.

She realized she was still fiddling with her sleeves and made herself stop. "I need to get over to Extension Sports. I promised Tanya I'd help out this afternoon."

"As long as you're sitting on a stool behind the counter, and not teaching climbing in the rock gym."

"Trust me," she assured as she stepped out of the curtained area, "I have *no* desire to get close to a rope right now." She sketched a wave and started to leave, but decided to swing by the cafeteria to grab a coffee on her way.

She was just fitting the lid on the tall cup when Cameron strode inside, heading straight for the hot-sandwich station. She hung back, not entirely certain why she didn't want to be noticed, but knowing that if she left now, he'd be sure to see her.

She cautiously sipped the strong brew, watching him over the top of the oversize cup.

The man did have a way of making plain blue jeans and an off-white fisherman's sweater look…extraordinary. And Faith knew she wasn't the only one who thought so, because there were plenty of female faces turning to watch Cameron's progress.

It was the middle of the afternoon, so the cafeteria was plenty busy, and several people spoke to him. Bits of conversation were audible above the clank of flatware and the hum of people's chatter. Everyone asked about Erik. Or the upcoming basketball game on Friday. He seemed to answer all comers, but he didn't exactly linger over them.

And that response wasn't altered whether or not the person to approach him was a man or a woman, she noted.

Then, when his tray was loaded with a plate of meat loaf, potatoes and salad, he didn't find a chair in the cafeteria, or head to the courtyard beyond the tall windows overlooking it. He simply pulled a thin wallet from his back pocket, flipped out a few bills for the cashier, and strode right back out of the cafeteria again, his demeanor neither welcoming nor standoffish.

She chewed the inside of her lip. What kind of a teacher would a man like that be? Stern, authoritative? Factual and removed? She certainly couldn't imagine him kicking back in his chair behind the large metal desk she remembered her high school teachers possessing, grinning in response to the rowdiness of a roomful of teenagers.

He was far too serious for that.

She walked out of the cafeteria, still watching him walking ahead of her, the tray held capably in his long-fingered hand.

She knew the man was strong. And she knew—having seen him in one of the worst situations a parent would ever find themselves—that he could be incredibly gentle with his son.

Realizing that she was still staring after him even when he'd entered the elevator for the second floor, she felt her cheeks heat and glanced around, hoping nobody noticed her hovering there in the corridor like some gawking groupie.

The fact was, she knew certain things about

Cameron and she was enormously curious to know more, and it wasn't *all* caused by the fact that her hormones had unfrozen with unseemly haste the first time she'd ever seen him.

But Cameron Stevenson was a family man, pure and simple.

So it didn't matter what sort of effect he had on her.

She wasn't going down *that* road ever again.

Chapter Five

"You came!"

There was a wealth of delight in Erik's young voice when Faith stuck her head in the door of his hospital room the next afternoon.

She pushed open the door wider, laughing a little. "Considering the way you've called me three times since this morning, did you think I'd forget?" Erik's first call had been at eight o'clock, and since then he'd gotten progressively more creative in his persuasive entreaty to visit him.

She hadn't had the heart to tell him that she'd planned to drop by all along. It might well have ruined his fun.

But her laugh hiccupped in her throat when she realized that Cameron was in the room, too. He was sitting in the corner, a stack of paper in his lap. For some reason, she'd expected him to be at the school.

"Hello."

"Ms. Taylor." He looked back down at the sheet, and began slashing his red pencil across it.

Faith pitied whoever the student was who'd completed that particular assignment. As for her, she felt pretty well dismissed, and didn't much care for the sensation.

But, she deliberately reminded herself, she hadn't come to see Cameron. She'd come to see Erik. So she focused on the boy. "How are you feeling today?"

He pulled a face. "They don't let me do nothing here. I don't see why I gotta stay here 'til tomorrow. I wanna go home now."

There were two chairs in the room, with Cameron occupying one. Yet she didn't feel comfortable enough to pull up the second, so she stood beside Erik's bed, instead. "They just want to make sure you're all healed up in here—" she lightly riffled her fingers through his mop of hair "—before you go climbing drainpipes."

"Drainpipes?"

"Don't give him ideas," Cam murmured from the corner.

"I'll tell you about 'em later," she whispered, sotto voce.

Erik grinned.

Cameron did not.

She eyed the video games still stacked beside Erik's

bed. "You have your games, at least, to keep you from getting bored."

"Dude, you got no idea how boring it is, though."

Dude? Her lips twitched. "I could bring you a book."

He looked askance and she laughed outright. "The horrors of it, huh? But I thought you liked going to the library for story time with Miss Emelda."

"I do. 'Cause she's got the best stories. But I don't gotta *read* them."

"Don't have to," Cameron corrected.

"Yeah. That."

Faith slid another surreptitious glance toward Cameron only to find his gaze *not* buried in his schoolwork, but firmly fixed on her. Wishing she would leave?

"Well. How do you feel about checkers?" She pulled out the travel game she'd stuck in her purse before coming to the hospital, and showed it to Erik.

"Cool." Erik scooted up on his pillows, folding his legs. "Can we play right now? Huh?"

She set the game on the mattress. "If it's all right with your dad." Cameron seemed to have gone very still and she lifted her eyebrows, giving the man plenty of opportunity to stop them. But he just nodded after a moment, then started scrawling with his red pencil again, his movements sharp.

Faith chewed the inside of her lip. His uncommonly stark expression tugged at her.

Erik noticed nothing amiss, though. His hands were busy as he unfolded the checkerboard right there on the bedding below his folded legs and doled out red and black checkers. "Come on, Faith."

She slowly perched her hip on the mattress. "I see you're not a novice, here."

"What's a novice?" His fingers rapidly placed the pieces—both hers and his.

"A beginner."

Erik laughed. "Me 'n' Dad play all the time."

"Guess it's a good thing we're not playing for money then." She couldn't help looking at Cameron again, adding another brushstroke to the painting of him in her mind. "Because I haven't played checkers in a really long time." Maybe Cameron didn't want anyone else playing the game with his son.

Yet that idea didn't feel right, either.

"You go first."

"I thought black went first?"

"Yeah, but you're the girl, so you gotta go first." Erik shook his head as if the matter were obvious.

"Well, I need all the help I can get against a regular player like you, so I'll take advantage of such chivalry." She slid a piece diagonally forward.

"What's chivalry?"

Dead, according to a good number of her friends. "It means being very courteous to women." She pushed another piece forward.

"Huh." Erik backed up his first piece with a second. "Dad says that's what we men gotta do."

Another unexpected brushstroke.

She blindly pushed another piece forward, which Erik immediately captured. He crowed and set her man on the blanket beside the board. After he made another capture, though, she decided she needed to pay a little closer attention. Erik's chivalry might have extended to allowing her the first move, but it certainly didn't extend to showing mercy once the game began.

Cameron watched Faith slowly fold up the sleeves of the khaki long-sleeved shirt that should have looked more official than appealing, and slide a little more fully onto the bed. He noticed her next move was made with far more deliberation than the previous ones.

He also noticed that Erik was thoroughly engrossed. His head hunched forward a little. Faith's blond head hunched forward a little. Their two heads didn't quite meet over the checkerboard, but it was close.

He set aside the math tests he was grading and rose, quietly leaving the room. Neither Faith nor Erik seemed to take note, and that was fine with him.

In the hall outside, he pressed his head back against the wall. There should've been an ache inside him. And because there wasn't, he found a new ache.

And he couldn't get the sight of their heads over the checkerboard out of his head no matter how hard he tried.

He wasn't sure how long he stood there when the door to Erik's room swished open and Faith touched his arm.

"Are you all right?"

He hadn't been all right since the day Laura died. "Needed to stretch my legs."

Her lashes lowered, hiding her expressive eyes. "I'm sorry if you think I've been…intrusive."

He straightened up at that. "Why would I think that?"

"Well—" she exhaled a little. "I can tell you don't really want me around here. But once Erik is released and back to normal, he'll quickly lose his fascination with me."

"I never said I didn't want you around." Irritation shortened his voice. If only that *were* the problem.

Her changeable eyes looked up at him at that. He could handle the curiosity and challenge glinting in them. But the vulnerability?

"Right," she returned. "That's why you glower every time I come within five feet of you and your son."

"I don't glower."

"You couldn't even say hello to me when I arrived."

"Erik gushed enough for both of us."

She huffed, skeptical. "Please. You also hated the toboggan yesterday. Thank goodness I didn't bring him a snowboard, which I strongly considered. Why don't you just admit it?"

"I don't hate it." He shoved his hands in his pockets. "I hate the fact that, no matter how hard I try to protect him, he still manages to get hurt. Okay?"

Her lips parted for a moment, then closed. "He's seven," she finally said. "He's bright and curious. Accidents can sometimes happen."

"And sometimes people don't survive them," he said flatly. "If you hadn't been there to get him out—" His throat closed. "I owe you. Okay? And I don't like owing anybody. Particularly when I should have prevented what happened in the first place. I should have known that Bodecker kid was filling Erik's head with stories. I shouldn't have taken Erik to the wedding in the first place. There're a lot of things I should have done, and I didn't." He wasn't speaking only of the past weekend, either. His should-haves went back a lot further than that.

She was silent, her eyes not entirely convinced.

"I used to play checkers with my wife. Erik's mother," he said abruptly. "In fact, on our first date, she prodded me into it." He'd come bearing tickets to the ballet, figuring the ethereal art lover whom he'd first spotted at a gallery showing would have been enchanted. Instead, they'd ended up sitting cross-legged on a checkered blanket in a city park, using the pattern on the blanket as the board, and torn pieces of French bread as their playing pieces, and he'd been the one enchanted.

"I'm sorry." Now, Faith looked stricken. "I had no idea."

How could she? And it wasn't the fact that another woman was playing checkers with his son that tore at him. It was the fact that looking at another woman playing checkers with his son had made him feel things he had no right to feel.

Even before the checkers, he'd felt things whenever Faith Taylor was in the vicinity. He didn't want to feel…anything.

"It's not you," he said gruffly. "I just—"

"—miss your wife," she finished softly.

He closed his eyes. He'd loved Laura. But he hadn't changed his life for her until after she was gone and it was too late.

Did he miss her?

He wasn't even sure of that anymore.

He scrubbed his hand down his face, leaving Faith to her assumption. "I need coffee."

"Frankly, you look like you need a good night's sleep more than you need caffeine," she countered evenly. "I suppose you don't want to *owe* the staff here at the hospital, either, for doing their jobs. What have you been doing? Staying with Erik around the clock?"

"Yeah. That's *my* job."

Her lips compressed. "And you'll be able to do it *so-o-o* well, when you're comatose from lack of sleep."

"I sleep."

"Where?"

"On a cot in Erik's room."

Her gaze drifted up and down his body, clearly taking a mental measurement. "Must be mighty comfortable," she said after a moment. "Is that why you had him put in a private room? So you could hover nearby 24/7?"

He'd requested a private room because that's what the Stevenson family did. Hell, when he'd been seven and getting his tonsils removed, his parents had not only had him in a private room, but with a private nurse, as well.

He pinched the bridge of his nose.

"Go get your coffee, Cameron," she murmured after a moment. "And some food. I'll stay here with Erik, if you think I can be trusted to keep him from harm, that is."

His breath hissed out between his teeth. "It's not a matter of trust, dammit."

Her eyebrows lifted. "Then what is it?"

How to admit to her reasonably posed question that he—a grown man—felt panicked nearly every time his son was out of eyeshot?

Faith waited, her heart squeezing at the shadows that darkened his eyes from melted chocolate to obsidian. "How do you take it?" she finally asked.

He looked at her. "What?"

"Your coffee." She lifted her hands when he started to shake his head. "Don't argue. I'm here. I might as well be of some use. And I'll bring back a milk shake or something for Erik, if that's all right."

The shadows slid behind sharp curiosity. "Why are you doing this?"

The question hovered between them for a moment. From down the hall, she could hear the rattle of a cart being rolled along the tile floor. Music was coming from a nearby room. The peds unit was decorated as cheerfully as any peds unit could be, but it was *still* a hospital.

Yet, as her brother had pointed out the other day, she'd entered the doors and ventured beyond the cafeteria.

Again.

Voluntarily.

"Truthfully," she said at length, "I have no idea. Maybe I just think Erik's a pretty terrific kid."

"He is." His jaw slanted. Centered. "Black. No sugar."

She should have guessed.

He started to pull out his wallet, but she waved her hand. "We'll settle up later." And before she could let her common sense tell her she was absolutely nuts for becoming even the slightest bit involved with the Stevenson men, she strode down the hall.

There was a faint itching at the base of her spine, and she knew that Cameron's gaze was following her.

Then she turned a corner and knowing she was out of range, she stopped. Drew in a deep breath and let it out slowly. Her heart was thudding.

It barely calmed down when she made it to the cafeteria and selected some items to take back to Erik's room. But, she figured wryly, if she were going to have a heart attack, at least she was in the right place to do it.

She thought she had herself more or less in control when she carried the tray back up to Erik's room. There was a good possibility her brother wouldn't much care for her bringing the boy the gargantuan chocolate milk shake, hamburger and French fries, but the boy's glee when she set them before him was worth any amount of trouble she might hear from Chris. And Cameron didn't put up any protests, either, when she handed him the tall coffee along with a plate of roast beef and all the fixin's.

"How'd you know I'd like roast beef?"

She lifted her shoulders. "Lucky guess," she demurred. There was no point in telling the man that she'd asked the cashier if Coach Stevenson had shown any particular preference beside the meat loaf that, if she hadn't been surreptitiously watching him the way she had the day before, she could have warned him to avoid.

"Eat up," she insisted when he didn't touch the food. "Before it gets cold."

"What about you, Faith?" Erik spoke around the French fry he was shoving into his mouth.

"Actually, I'm meeting a friend for an early dinner."

"Are you gonna go now then?" He eyed the checkerboard. "Or can we play another game?"

"You've already trounced me at two. But maybe we can play another time."

"Yeah. After you come t'bogganing with me. Can *you* toboggan?"

"Questioning my prowess because I'm a girl?"

He wrinkled his nose. "Huh?"

She laughed. "Yes, I can really toboggan. And snowboard, for that matter. Can't say I'm expert by any means, though. I'd actually rather have skis on my feet than do either."

"Dad likes to ski, doncha, Dad?"

"What about *you*?"

Erik shook his head. "Never gone. Dad went b'fore Christmas, though, huh, Dad?"

"What did you do while he skied?"

Erik rolled his eyes. "Visited Grandma and Grandpa in Denver. They had me go to a party."

Which sounded like a fate worse than death, judging by his tone. And Faith couldn't help but wonder if Cameron had skied alone, or if he'd had company that he hadn't wanted his son interfering with.

Her mood turned south.

"Well, like I said, I've got an early dinner. So I'll catch you on the flip side, 'kay?" She lifted her hand and Erik high-fived it. "Take care, sweetie." She winked at him, letting her gaze skate over the boy's father, and sped out the door.

She hurried through the pediatric wing before she could come up with some reason to stay. Her feet dragged a little when she passed the nursery with its wide window overlooking the collection of bassinets. A nurse sat in a rocking chair, crooning to the tiny baby in her arms.

Faith paused, watching. A frazzled-looking young man joined her at the window after a few minutes. He stared through the glass with disbelief and adoration all rolled into one.

"Which one is yours?"

He pointed. "Baby girl. Last one on the right." He shook his head. "Don't even have a girl's name picked out, because my wife was so convinced it would be a boy."

Judging by his expression, Faith figured the man was not in the least disappointed. "Congratulations."

"Thanks. What about you?"

She shook her head. "I'm just admiring."

"My wife used to do that, too, before she got pregnant." He pressed his hand against the window. The nurse noticed him and beckoned, and he practically tripped over his feet in his haste to go in and visit his daughter.

Sighing a little, Faith turned to go as he fumbled

into a protective gown and the nurse transferred the baby from the bassinet into his arms.

Admiring was all she would ever do.

"D'ya think she's got a boyfriend?"

Cameron propped his feet on the end of Erik's hospital bed. On the television hanging from the wall, college basketball was in full force. "Does who have a boyfriend?" The question was for show. He knew exactly whom Erik was referring to.

"Jeez, Dad. Get a clue."

He lifted an eyebrow. "I have no idea if Ms. Taylor has a boyfriend." Didn't mean he hadn't wondered plenty about it himself. Not that he intended to apprise his inquisitive seven-year-old of that fact.

"You could ask Dr. Taylor," Erik suggested. "He'd know 'cause she's his sister. I wonder what it's like to have a sister?"

Cam shrugged. "Can't help you there. Never had one." Nor a brother.

"Did my mom have a sister?"

Cam's gaze slid from the television to Erik. "No. Your mother was an only child, too." One of the things they'd had in common.

"Am I gonna get to go home for real tomorrow?"

Long used to his son's ping-pong method of bouncing from topic to topic, Cam nodded.

"Good." Erik's knees bounced. "I don't gotta go back to school yet, though?"

Cam gave Erik a dry stare that his boy interpreted just fine.

"If I see Tommy Bodecker in the halls, I'm gonna pound him."

Cam made a noncommittal sound. Truth was, his son didn't have a violent bone in him. Erik didn't even squash bugs. He was more interested in collecting them and giving them names.

"She's real pretty, huh?"

"Yeah."

"Not pretty like Mom."

Cam closed his eyes. The clear image of Laura that should've been there wasn't. He opened his eyes again, and stared blindly at the television. "Your mother had hair as black as midnight and eyes the color of lilacs." She'd been barely five feet tall, with an eye-popping hourglass figure. Kissing her had generally been most easily accomplished if he simply lifted her up to him.

That wouldn't be such a problem with Faith. Her head reached his shoulder. He'd just have to lean down a little. She'd lean up a little.

The thoughts snuck in. Grabbed hold, good and tight, not so willing to be shook.

"I know. I got Mom's picture in my bedroom," Erik said. "Just Faith's all…kinda…gold."

Cam's hand curled. Golden. She was that. "Yeah. You gonna finish that milk shake or not?"

Erik snatched up the oversize cup. "Yes," he said protectively, and tucked the straw between his teeth for good measure.

Relieved to have distracted his son, Cam focused once more on the ball game.

Too bad his mind wasn't as easily swayed as his son's.

Faith *was* golden. Gleaming blond hair, gleaming brown-green eyes. Gleaming golden skin, satin smooth and sleek with lean muscles and long limbs.

Dammit.

Chapter Six

Every inch of every bleacher inside Thunder Canyon High School's gymnasium was occupied that Friday night. The heat generated by all the bodies was more than enough to keep the enormous building warmed, as two teams battled it out on the hardwood for top spot in the state basketball semifinals.

Todd Gilmore, star center, stood on the foul line, bouncing the ball a few times, preparing to take his second free throw that would put his team in a tie game. Only ninety seconds remained on the clock.

Feet pounded collectively on the metal bleachers, creating a racket loud enough to wake the heavens. Gilmore's name was a throbbing chant on the air.

Faith, sitting in the nosebleed section—second row

from the top—peered down to the sideline where
Cameron stood, his attention intently focused on his
players. The long sleeves of his white shirt were folded
up over his forearms. His narrow gray tie was pulled
loose of his collar. His thick hair was slightly rumpled.
He gave no indication whatsoever that he even noticed
the raucous crowd.

Todd set up for his throw, the basketball rolling
smoothly from the tips of his fingers in a graceful arc
toward the basket.

It sank right through, and the crowd went ballistic.

The man to Faith's right crowed. "Nothing but net!"

Faith smiled, still watching Cameron.

Erik stood on the bench behind him, right behind
the players on his father's team. He had an enormous
foam finger on his hand that he waved about wildly.
She knew he'd been released from the hospital on
Wednesday as scheduled, because she'd seen him and
Cameron leaving as *she* was leaving, having grabbed
a sandwich with her brother for lunch that day in the
cafeteria, and she'd watched their departure from her
SUV parked in the lot.

She still wasn't sure if that had been cowardice on
her part, or common sense.

But Erik had noticed her, and waved until she'd
feared he'd fall out of the wheelchair he'd had to use
until reaching Cameron's car.

Now, Faith couldn't tear her attention away from
Erik's dad.

Cameron clapped his hands together as the game
continued, frenzied. He called out to his players. Faith

could see him glance up at the clock as if the depleting seconds were of no consequence. Up the court the players pounded. A bank shot, deflected. Down the court again.

The crowd was on its feet.

The noise was deafening.

How long could it take for ninety seconds to pass?

Faith pressed her fist to her mouth, her heart in her throat, just as caught up in the game as everyone else. She could see Bobby Romano in the stands, his expression dark as he looked at his son, Danny, on the sidelines, still benched.

The ball whizzed from player to player. The seconds cranked down. Twelve. Eleven. Ten.

"Come on. Come on." Her gaze slanted down again to Cameron. His hands were on his hips, his feet planted. She could practically see him willing his boys through their play.

Seven. Six. Five.

The ball flew. Hit the backboard. Bounced off the rim.

Players scrambled, rebounded.

Slammed the ball home.

The buzzer sounded.

And the crowd erupted, people pouring onto the court.

Cam's team had won.

Faith blew out a long breath, her heart pounding. She sat down, her legs weak.

"Helluva game!" The man beside her was positively gleeful. "Helluva game! First time we've made it to the state championship in seventeen years!"

She laughed. Her gaze kept sliding down to where Cameron stood. He'd lifted Erik up onto his shoulder and the boy was waving his foam finger over his head. Parents and players milled around, a congestion of jubilation on their side of the court, while the opponent's side rapidly emptied. She gathered up her coat and started making her way down the steps.

"Faith. Faith!" Erik's voice managed to find form among the loud roar.

She waved at him and angled her steps diagonally toward him. Her heart thudded unevenly. The players were whooping and hollering, slapping each other on their backs, and she couldn't help but laugh at their exuberance. She also couldn't get any closer to Erik than the second to bottom bleacher. "Good game!"

Erik's smile practically reached around the back of his head. "When are you gonna come tobogganing?"

Faith lifted her shoulders. "Whenever your dad says you're up to it."

Erik wriggled around until he got his dad's attention. Cameron tipped him off his shoulder, making the boy giggle before his feet hit the bleacher next to Faith.

"Did you see me wave at you when I got outta the hospital?"

Faith bent her knee on the bleacher so she was closer to his level. "You saw me wave back, right?"

"How come you didn't come and see me?"

She pulled out her pager and held it up for him to see. "I was on call. A skier got lost." That was the truth. She'd hovered in the hospital parking lot longer than she ought to have, in fact.

"Did you rescue him like you did me?"

"Well, he was a lot easier to find than *you* were," she assured.

"Did ya' hear that there's *gold* in the mine? All 'cause of me falling in?"

Faith laughed. "Well, that ought to drive Tommy Bodecker clean out of his tree."

Erik grinned, grabbing her hand. He was still practically yelling to be heard over the din. "You gotta come with us to The Hitching Post. Dad *never* lets me go there, but he's gonna tonight, 'cause we won. Says I'm his good-luck charm, so he's gotta."

"Naturally, a good-luck charm should *always* be included in the after-game celebration."

"So, will you?"

She started to shake her head, but Cameron leaned over just then. "Come on along," he invited.

Her heart jolted. She tried to tell herself it was just surprise, but she wasn't convinced.

"Everybody's going," he continued.

Of course. She ordered her heart to settle right back down again. Fat lot of good it did, though.

"I know it's late, but I owe you a dinner," Cameron added unexpectedly. The people standing between them were finally shuffling out of the way and Cameron scooped up an enormous duffel bag packed with sports equipment. He looped the strap over his shoulder and looked up, his gaze meeting hers. "What do you say?"

Heat squiggled along her veins.

"Please?" Erik wriggled her arm.

He's a family man. A family man. A family man.

"I...sure." She exhaled the word, ignoring the frantic reminder circling inside her head.

Cameron nodded. "Meet you there. Hustle up, Erik."

Faith blinked as Erik scrambled down from the bleachers and hurried to catch up with his dad's long-legged stride. The squiggles were still squiggling, even though she couldn't have said whether or not Cameron was pleased she'd agreed.

"That is one seriously good-looking man."

Faith jerked around to see Tanya smirking at her. "I didn't know you were here."

"I didn't know *you* were here," her friend returned. "So...what gives?" Her eyebrows rose meaningfully.

"Nothing gives. Did you close the store tonight?"

"Yup. No point in staying open when all the sports fans were here. Derek's on duty and Toby is spending the night at a friend's. All of which I mentioned at dinner the other day. When you did not mention that you were coming to the game tonight."

Faith stepped off the bleachers. Tanya followed. "I wasn't planning to," she admitted.

"Just couldn't help yourself, huh?" Tanya bumped her shoulder to Faith's when she didn't reply. "Hey. I'm just teasing you, you know. Because it's pretty nice to see you showing some interest in a man. After you split up with Jess—"

"I'm not interested," Faith said hastily.

Tanya just eyed her and the defensiveness oozed out of Faith, leaving her feeling deflated.

They pushed through the gymnasium doors and followed the clusters of people heading to their cars. "He's not the kind of man for me," she said after a moment.

"Why on earth not?" Tanya sidled in front of her, and stopped, forcing Faith to stop as well. "Sweetie, you're my best friend. Talk to me."

Words welled up inside Faith, but they were held back by a dam of her own making. "I'm not interested in *any* kind of man," she rephrased. "Yet—" she added hastily, recognizing the glint in her friend's determined blue eyes.

Tanya tucked her arm through Faith's. "Well, that's something, at least. You want to come over and have coffee and cake? Derek was baking again on his day off. Death by Chocolate. Seriously good stuff."

"Tempting." It was. Derek's prowess in the kitchen was significant. And he had a way with chocolate that generally made him the designated chef at the fire station when he was on duty. "But I can't." They neared her SUV and she tugged out her keys.

"Early shift tomorrow?"

"Um, no." Though she was on call, as she usually was.

Tanya was eyeing her again. "Okay. What's up?"

Faith unlocked her truck and tossed her purse inside. She tugged on the scarf hanging around her neck. "I, um, I told Erik I'd drop by The Hitching Post after the game."

"Erik, or Erik's fine-looking daddy?"

"Tanya—"

Her friend grinned. "Oh, fine. I'll let you off the hook. But one of these days, you're just gonna have to admit to me that you've got the hots for Cameron Stevenson." Tanya squeezed her arm and stepped back from the vehicle. "It's okay, you know. You don't have to be ashamed of it. You're a healthy, twenty-nine-year-old woman. Enjoy it." She started to cross the lot, but turned back after a few feet. "By the way, I'm going to want details!"

Faith felt herself flush, and Tanya laughed, as she darted between the slow-moving cars. Faith climbed into her SUV, only to sit there for a good ten minutes before the congestion in the parking lot eased. Ten minutes during which she seriously considered turning left out of the lot and driving straight home.

But when she nosed out of the lot, the SUV seemed to turn right of its own accord.

The Hitching Post was located in Old Town, down the street from The Hall. The parking lot behind the building was already bulging with cars, so she parked down the block and walked back to the popular grill. As she walked beyond the old-fashioned hitching post outside the building, she couldn't help but remember the frantic night she'd spent searching for Erik.

But when she pushed through the door, she pushed aside those thoughts. Erik Stevenson was standing on a bar stool, near the original bar from when the establishment was once a saloon, putting him at the same height as his dad's tallest player, and making him easily visible through the crowd.

She crossed the hardwood floor, heading his way.

Country music throbbed through the place. She had to turn this way and that to slip between groups of people crowded around the bar tables, and nearly fell on her rear when a young man backed straight into her.

He hurriedly steadied her, and she smiled off his humorous apology, only to turn around and find Cameron standing two inches behind her.

And she felt truly unsteady in that moment as every nerve she possessed went on alert.

"I was beginning to wonder if you were going to show." His fingers wrapped around her arm and even through her coat she felt the jolt of it. "Come on. I've got a table over here." He guided her through the throng, his tall body close behind hers, and she dragged in a breath, surreptitiously pressing her palm to her swaying stomach.

The table was nearly in the corner, and an enormous basket of cheese-covered fries sat in the center of it. Cam scooped Erik off the bar stool and carried him—one arm around the waist—over to the table, and dumped him on a chair. The boy could hardly seem to stop laughing, and his high spirits were so infectious that she relaxed a little and managed to slide into the chair that Cameron pulled out for her without completely embarrassing herself.

Which didn't mean that she didn't nearly jump out of her skin when he touched her shoulders. She looked up at him.

"Your coat?"

Her cheeks heated. He was only trying to help her out of her coat. Her thoughts skidded and she hurriedly unbuttoned the big round buttons on the front and shrugged out of the navy wool peacoat. He tossed it on the fourth chair that already held an assortment of winter wear. Then he sat down in the chair to her right. The square table was spacious enough, but his legs brushed against hers as he scooted in.

"Sorry," he murmured, and angled his legs in another direction.

Faith hurriedly snatched up one of the menus sitting on the center of the table and studied it, even though she'd eaten at The Hitching Post often enough to have the entire thing memorized. "Have you and Erik already ordered?"

Cameron plucked a few crispy fries from the basket. "Only these." He pulled them free of the melted cheese topping them.

Her stomach dipped again as she watched him consume them, then lick his thumb before wiping his hands with his napkin.

"Get you something to drink?" The pregnant waitress who stopped by their table was young. Fairly new to town, too, Faith knew, courtesy of Tanya, who kept her finger pretty firmly on the town's pulse. The petite Latina looked busy, but her sparkling eyes and smile didn't show how harried she undoubtedly felt as she waited patiently.

Faith's gaze skated over Cameron's beer and Erik's soda. "I'll just have water, thanks."

"I'll be right back with that. Give you a chance to look over the menu." She hurried off.

Even though the place was crammed with people

and noise, Faith felt very alone there at the table with Cameron and Erik. It wasn't necessarily an unpleasant sensation. Erik was slurping his soda through his straw, blowing bubbles as much as drinking, and Cameron was working on the cheese fries with an oddly intense determination.

She wasn't going to blindly study the menu any longer, and she flipped it closed. "Amazing game tonight."

Cameron's eyes slanted her way for a moment. "Yeah. Haven't seen you at any of the games before."

She repositioned the napkin in her lap. "Guess I got caught up in the excitement like the rest of Thunder Canyon. It's on to the state championship now. Quite an accomplishment on your part." His lashes were unreasonably thick, she noticed, not for the first time.

"I'd feel more accomplished if the guys were pulling better grades in math." His lips twisted wryly. "Basketball's just a game."

She leaned forward a little. "Better keep your voice down when you say stuff like that. Lynching isn't too far in Thunder Canyon's past, you know."

His head tilted and she sucked in her breath, painfully aware of how close they sat. Fortunately, the waitress returned with her water, and Faith sat back, wrapping her unsteady hand around the glass as they gave their orders and the waitress headed off once more. "So, is the championship on Friday?"

He shook his head. "We'll have next week off. Game's the following week. Superstition or something, but nobody wanted to schedule a game on Friday the thirteenth."

She'd forgotten all about the date. She was due to have lunch on Valentine's Day with a bunch of girlfriends. "I imagine you must have played basketball yourself?"

He nodded, and looked up when Mayor Brookhurst stopped by, clapping him on the back for the great game. He stood and shook the man's hand. "Tell that to the team." Cam easily deflected the mayor's praise. "They're the ones who worked their tails off for it."

The mayor smiled broadly, obviously feeling expansive. "Don't be modest now, Coach. Considering what you've accomplished with a bunch of teenagers, imagine what we could do if you were on the town council."

Cameron's smile stayed put, but Faith could tell it was forced. She'd seen for herself that Cam didn't always agree with mayoral opinions. "I'm considering it," he admitted, without giving away much.

The mayor nodded, satisfied enough, and moved along, evidently happy to keep greeting the elated crowd as if he were personally responsible for the night's outcome.

Erik was wriggling in his seat, his soda already gone.

Faith laughed a little, watching him. "You're like a Mexican jumping bean over there, Mister Erik. I think I may need to start calling you Juan or something."

"I never had Mexican jumping beans. But Susie in school did. But she got 'em taken away 'cause the teacher said she was playing with 'em during class. They're so-o-o cool. Dad, have we ever been to Mexico?"

Cameron shook his head as he sat down again. He handed Erik a handful of coins. "Here. Go play a video game."

"Aw-w-wright." Erik scooped up the coins and dashed off to the arcade area behind their table.

Cameron's gaze followed after his son, then he looked back at Faith. "Be nice to bottle some of that energy. I could use it to perk up my sixth-hour class every day." He nudged the basket of fries toward her. "Have some."

Her mouth was pretty much watering and it was easier to blame it on the cheese fries than anything else, so she took advantage of the offer.

"What were you like in school?"

Faith shrugged, and wiped her fingers on her napkin. "Anxious to graduate," she supplied wryly.

His lips tilted and the crease in his cheek deepened.

She took a quick drink of water. Set down the glass, only to rotate it between her thumb and forefinger. "I couldn't wait to leave Thunder Canyon, actually. I didn't really think anybody could have any sort of real life here."

His gaze centered on the fries, hiding his expression. "You were young, and the town is pretty small. What'd you do?"

"I went off to New Mexico for college. Met someone. Graduated. Got married. Got divorced." She shrugged. "Nothing particularly interesting." *Just life-altering,* the voice inside her head whispered.

He was silent for a moment and she looked up from her water glass to find his gaze on her. "What about you?" she asked somewhat desperately. "What brought you to Thunder Canyon? I think I heard that you were from Colorado, right?"

"Denver. My wife drove through here once and fell in love with the place."

She bent her elbow on the table, and propped her chin on her hand. Jess had never done anything simply because *she'd* loved it. "And you moved here because of that?" How much he must have loved his wife.

"She'd just had Erik. She wanted to raise him here, rather than in the city."

"I guess I've never thought of Denver as being all that major of a city."

His lips twitched. "Better not let any of the Denver power brokers hear you say that."

She lifted her glass, amused. "I think I might be safe all the way over here in Thunder Canyon. Are you really going to run for town council? You're always at the meetings."

"So are you."

"Ah, but I'm a county employee who has to report back to her team anything that might affect our ability to scrounge space from the town services. Only reason we can afford to have the team spread out the way we are is through cooperation with the local agencies that share their resources—and office space—with us. Every time the budget gets looked at, we sweat it."

"The council supports your presence, though."

She nodded. "True. Some members of the police department aren't so enamored of my presence, but it usually works out in the end."

"Well." His hand closed over hers, and her heart simply stopped for a moment. "I, for one, am damn glad you were here." His thumb brushed over the back of her hand and the chaos surrounding them seemed to fade away.

Then he let go of her, reaching for the cheese fries again, and the chaos returned, loud and rambunctious as ever.

Faith dropped her hands to her lap, rubbing one hand over the tingling in the other. A happy father stopped by to pound Cameron on the back, then Erik dashed over, and a slightly shorter boy followed hard in his wake.

"Hey, Dad. Can I spend the night at Josh's? His mom's over there. She said I could."

Cameron shook his head without even seeming to think about the matter. "Tell Mrs. Lampson thanks, but no."

Faith felt the disappointment sweeping through Erik even before his shoulders sank. "Come on, Dad."

Cameron merely lifted an eyebrow, and Erik's pleading stopped before it had barely begun. "Have you spent all of your change?"

"No, sir."

"Better do it now before the food gets served, then."

Erik nodded. He turned and shuffled off with Josh at his side.

Cameron didn't look at her, but pulled another few fries free of the web of cheese.

"Excuse me." Faith stood and dropped her napkin on her seat. "I'll be right back."

She felt Cameron's gaze on her spine as she went after Erik. He was feeding coins into a video game, his expression sulky, when she crouched down beside him. "I have some free time tomorrow," she told him. "Around ten. I could come by and we can check out that toboggan of yours. What do you say, Juan?"

His eyes, so similar to his father's, brightened. "Honest?"

She stuck out her hand. "Honest."

He slapped his palm against hers. The game beside them chirped and gurgled. And Faith resumed her seat at the table with Cameron.

"What was that about?"

"I told Erik I'd come tobogganing with him tomorrow." She eyed him. "Unless that's something you're going to say no to as well?"

He sat back in his seat. "You think I should've let him spend the night at the Lampsons'."

"Would it have been so terrible?"

"Maria Lampson works a swing shift every night at a convenience store. She leaves Josh home alone with his twelve-year-old sister from midnight to 8:00 a.m. So, no, I'm not going to feel badly for disappointing Erik."

"I didn't realize."

"Now you do."

They sat there, eyeing each other.

Then the waitress, Juliet, appeared with a laden tray and began unloading their dinner.

Erik darted back to the table, and slid onto his seat, nearly diving headfirst into his hamburger. "Faith's gonna come tobogganing with me," he announced. A drop of ketchup dripped onto his chin.

Cam watched Faith lean over and hand Erik's napkin to him. His son took it and wiped his face without breaking stride for a second, and without adding his usual complaints whenever Cam told him to use his napkin.

"We could use the hill behind our house, right, Dad? It's big enough."

The hill was steep as hell. And he really didn't want his son going near it. But Faith's gaze was fixed on his face as if waiting for him to deny Erik another pleasure, and he choked down the misgivings. "It's big enough," he finally said.

Faith's long, soft lashes swept down and her lips looked ready to soften into a smile.

He'd spent more than enough time being preoccupied over Faith Taylor's lips.

It wasn't as if he was going to do something about his curiosity over whether they were as supple as they looked.

He made himself look away, only to realize the troublesome threesome were bearing down on him, intent glinting in their overly made-up eyes. Tiffany Scherer, Amber Wells and Krista Decker. Pretty girls with too much time on their hands.

He stifled an oath.

Faith leaned a little closer. "What's wrong?"

He grabbed her hand and hauled her out of her chair. "Dance with me."

"What?" Her napkin slid to the hardwood floor.

He knew Erik was staring at them, goggle-eyed. "Dance with me," he repeated, and nearly lifted her off her feet to get her onto the dance floor that was only sparsely occupied. He swung her into his arms, glancing over her head.

The teenaged girls had halted their progress, expressions of surprise etched in triplicate across their faces.

"God help their fathers," he muttered.

Faith was staring at him as if he'd lost his mind. And maybe he had lost it. Because he could feel every inch of her lithe body—clad in a bronze turtleneck that made her hair look more golden than ever and narrow brown jeans that made her legs look longer than ever— against his body. "*Whose* fathers?"

He shuffled, turning her so she could see the girls. "Their fathers. You know what it's like to be chased by three seventeen-year-old girls? It's a bloody nightmare."

A soft laugh erupted from her and he felt the ripple of it through his chest. "They have a crush on you, I take it."

He could feel his neck heating. "I don't know. Just every time I turn around, there they are. It's becoming…a problem."

"Because you like them?"

He glared at her. "Give me a break. They're children."

She shifted against him, her hand slipping up over his shoulder. Their legs brushed against each other as they slowly moved over the postage stamp of a dance area. "Poor guy."

"You wouldn't find it so amusing if it were *you*. They've been bringing me cranberry muffins every school day lately. I don't even like cranberries."

She considered that. "Romantic gestures. Well, I suppose if it were me, I probably wouldn't find it funny, either. But since I've never had young men falling over themselves for me—or grown men, for that matter—I can't be entirely certain."

That seemed inconceivable to Cam. He was vaguely aware of the girls turning on their collective heels. "At least they're not in any of my classes this semester. I don't know how to discourage them anymore than I already have."

"Get a girlfriend," she said smoothly.

"I'm—" he broke off. Married, he'd almost said.

Only he wasn't married. He was alone.

And he had a beautiful woman who was very much alive in his arms, her body warming his.

"You're what?"

"Hungry," he said abruptly. "And our food's getting cold." He stopped doing the shuffle-disguised-as-a-dance, and nudged her back toward the table.

He'd accomplished one thing at least—diverting the trio of girls, even if it was momentary.

Too bad he'd also accomplished something else.

Awakening a hunger of another sort that, up until now, he'd managed to keep under control.

He sat down in the seat, dropping the napkin over his jeans that had gone painfully tight.

"I never seen you dance before, Dad."

"Finish your hamburger, Erik."

"But—"

"Then you can order dessert."

Erik nearly shoved the rest of the hamburger into his mouth, his eyes gleaming at the prospect.

Cam, however, couldn't look at Faith without wishing he were feasting on *her*.

As soon as she'd picked up her fork, though, she jumped a little. "My pager," she said, and pulled it off her belt, peering at the display.

Erik craned around, trying to get a look. Faith flashed him the display, and cast Cameron a look that was too hard to read. "I'm sorry. I'm going to have to run."

"Everything okay?"

"Yeah. Just duty calling." She rose and started pulling on her coat. He stood also, helping her despite the surprised look she gave him. She gestured at the table. "Sorry about the meal."

If he hadn't dragged her onto the dance floor, she'd have had a chance to eat more of the mammoth salad she'd ordered than just a few bites. "We could get it packed for you to take."

"I won't have a chance to get to it," she murmured. "But thanks. I'm…sorry about this."

So was he, he thought, watching her walk out of The Hitching Post.

More sorry than he had any right to be.

Chapter Seven

Faith sat in her car, looking up at Cameron and Erik's home. There were only two other homes on the hillside, set well apart from each other. And it reminded her all over again that Cameron hadn't always been a high school coach and math teacher. He'd had an entirely different career before he'd come to Thunder Canyon. One that, judging by the spacious size and rugged beauty of the house, must have paid pretty darn well.

She had a fleeting urge to put the car in gear and turn around and run. But Erik had already thrown open the wide front door and was racing pell-mell down the shoveled walkway toward her, the toboggan clutched under his arm. He ran all the way to the street and looked fit to vibrate out of his skin as he waited for her to join him on the sidewalk.

"Hello," she greeted. "What's your name again?"

Erik's dimples flashed. "Juan."

She nodded. "Right. I remember. And that thing?" She tapped the end of the rolled sled. "That's a mechanical bull, isn't it?"

"A *real* one," Erik corrected.

"Erik." Cameron stood on the front porch. "Invite Ms. Taylor in."

Faith's stomach jittered. Nerves soothed by Erik came back in full force with the presence of his father. "That's okay," she raised her voice so he could hear. "The hill behind your house should be perfect for this puppy." He could hover as close as he needed.

"Master Juan?" She looked at Erik as she pulled her gloves out of her coat pocket, and snugged her scarf tighter around her neck. "Think you'd better put some boots on those feet of yours."

He looked down. Giggled. Flew back up the walk in his stockinged feet, darting past his dad into the house.

Faith retrieved Cam's coat from her car and slowly followed, since Cameron was still standing there. She took her time pulling on her gloves. Maybe if she didn't look at him, she wouldn't spend another night plagued with dreams about him.

Right.

"Nice place you have," she commented, stopping near the base of the five stone steps leading up to a front door that could have accommodated her car it was so wide. She tossed the coat to him.

"It's a roof." He neatly caught the garment.

She wriggled her toes inside her boots. From inside the house, she heard Erik's yell, asking where his snow boots were.

Cameron's gaze met hers and his lips tilted. "Better come inside," he suggested dryly. "Based on previous experience, this may take a while. He was supposed to have gathered up his stuff before you got here."

He stepped back, waiting.

It was just a house, she told herself. And he was just a tall man in blue jeans and a thick wheat-colored sweater.

Didn't make going up the steps and walking past him any less disturbing, though.

And he smelled good. Again.

She swallowed and focused somewhat desperately on the house. From the foyer was a wide-open view of the land behind the house, courtesy of the plate glass windows that seemed to take the place of walls. Her feet rooted into place at the magnificence of it. "A little *more* than a roof."

His hand lightly touched the small of her back and she nearly jumped forward a foot. "It's the view that sold us on the house."

Now, her spine was tingling. "I'll bet."

"Da-ad!"

He let out a breath. "Excuse me." He dumped the coat on the already-laden coatrack near the door.

She nodded and he disappeared down a hall. She could hear the low tone of his voice as he directed Erik's search. She could have stood there looking out those windows for hours. The snowy hillside looked pristine, the white powder glittering like jewels beneath the clear, afternoon sun.

Beyond the foyer and the soaring great room furnished with oversize, rustic pine, the floor plan split, going down a half-dozen steps to the kitchen with a built-in breakfast nook, and a less formal family room. Looked like Cam used it more for an office though, judging by the textbooks and papers strewn across a desk that floated in the middle of the room, facing out the windows.

She wondered how he accomplished any work. If she had a view like his, she'd have to face away from it, because there was no way she could have concentrated.

Erik and Cam were still searching, evidently, and she passed the desk, hoping her intense interest was masked by casual glances. There were a few framed photos of Erik sitting on a bookshelf. And no photos of his mother as far as she could tell.

Her curiosity over the woman who still held Cameron's heart would have to go unquenched.

"Okay. He's ready." Cameron stepped into view, closely followed by Erik. The boy ran across the room and shoved at one of the windows. It slid silently aside, then started to close as soon as Erik reached the covered deck right outside. Cam stopped it from closing altogether, though, holding it open with the palm of his hand.

Faith went outside. She couldn't see a single fingerprint on the glass pane and couldn't help but wonder how they managed that. "You coming?"

He jerked his chin at the mess on his desk. "Kids complain about homework, but it's the teachers who really get socked with it."

She nodded. But a glance at his hand told her he wasn't as calm as he seemed.

His knuckles were white.

"It's just a sled. We'll be careful," she said quietly.

His gaze was focused beyond her, and she wondered what he was seeing. "If I thought otherwise, you wouldn't be here," he assured.

She supposed that was a compliment, and went to the side of the deck where a short staircase led to the ground and Erik waited, standing on top of the toboggan.

Faith studied the lie of the hill. The tree line didn't pick up until well beyond the base of the hill, and beyond the trees was the road. It couldn't have been a more perfect location if she'd taken Erik out to the hill behind the skating rink where most kids congregated for sledding.

"Alrighty, Juan. Let's take a crack at this, shall we? We'll go down together until you get the knack of steering, and then you can fly solo. Right?"

Cam was grateful there were no witnesses nearby when he broke out in a sweat at Erik's first faltering attempt on the toboggan. Faith had already accompanied him down the hill more than once, with Erik tucked securely in front of her, and her sleek ponytail streaming behind them until they disappeared from his line of vision.

He went into the kitchen, shoving the bench in the breakfast nook out of his way. The angle was different there, and he could see clear to the snow-filled ravine at the base of the hill.

On Erik's solo attempt, his son made it about ten feet before he tipped sideways, rolling like some human snowball in the snow. Faith, perched farther down the hill, darted upward, her boots sinking into the snow, and when she caught Erik up, Cam could hear their laughter ringing on the afternoon. She flipped a handful of loose snow into his son's face and settled him back on his feet, pointing to the top of the hill again.

Cam slid back a foot, not necessarily wanting to be seen with his nose pressed against the window like some starving kid at a candy store. Erik plodded back up the hill, dragging the sled behind him by the nylon cord.

On his third attempt, he made it all the way to the base of the hill, and the *whoop* his son made could've been heard in the next county. Cam could see him pumping his arm in the air, strutting around victoriously. Then Erik grabbed the toboggan again and raced up the hill.

He spotted Cam watching and waved wildly. "Dad. Watch me!"

Cam lifted his hand in return. At the base of the hill, Faith looked up in his direction.

Then she smiled.

He was vaguely surprised the warmth of it didn't melt the snow all around her.

"Watch me," Erik cried again, and was off in a blur of neon green. Again, when he made it to the base, he bounded to his feet to dance around like he'd won Olympic gold. Then some lively discussion ensued, and Faith trudged to the top of the hill, the sled tucked under her arm.

She didn't look toward the window, where she had to know he was still watching, and he wondered if it was deliberate or not.

She arranged her lithe form on the toboggan, long legs crossed in front of her. Cam caught a flash of her grin in the moment gravity took hold and she went flying down the hill.

Cam turned his back on the sight and returned to his work, but it wasn't so easy to turn his back on the feelings churning inside him.

He stared at the textbooks in front of him. At the rate he was going, he'd be using the same final exam this year as he'd given to his students last.

Through the insulated windows, he could still hear Erik's and Faith's laughter.

He abruptly shut the books, went out to the mudroom located below the kitchen, shrugged into a down vest, and went outside.

The snowball smacked him in the center of his chest, and exploded into powder.

"Bull's-eye," Erik crowed. He pranced around victoriously in the snow. "I told you he'd come out here, Faith. Dad *loves* the snow."

"Good thing." She waved her arm at the snowy landscape. "Because this isn't exactly the Mojave Desert."

Cam straightened, a snowball in his hand. He lobbed it at his son, catching Erik in the shoulder. His boy laughed, and dove down. And Cam realized belatedly that Erik and Faith had already prepared an arsenal.

The snowballs came fast and furious. Almost as fast as Erik's laughter.

Faith was no help, either. She was most definitely in his son's corner.

And she had a hell of an arm on her, though she left most of the work to Erik.

"You're gonna regret this," he warned, deflecting a hail of snowballs with his arm.

She laughed, and handed Erik another snowball.

Cam ducked his head and dove straight toward them, tackling them both into the soft snow.

Erik wriggled out from beneath his arm and jumped on his back, trying to shove snow down the collar of his shirt. Cam yelped, twisting around. He grabbed Erik and tipped him upside down.

Erik laughed so hard he looked ready to bust. "Get him, Faith. Help me!"

But Faith was still lying on her back in the snow, her legs and arms splayed, laughing herself.

Cam shoveled a handful of snow down his son's collar and let the boy go. Erik jumped around screaming like a banshee, trying to shake the snow out.

"Monkey," Cam said and turned to extend a hand to Faith.

She took it and he pulled her to her feet, only to have her shove a handful of snow into his face.

Erik sat down on his butt and howled. "She did it, she did it!"

Cam swiped a hand down his face. "You two planned this, then? If one of you couldn't get me, the other one would?" He bared his teeth, holding back his own laughter.

Faith was backing away, her palms held out peaceably. "Just some good, clean fun," she assured, breathlessly.

"Good *cold* fun, more like."

Erik got to his feet and grabbed the toboggan. "I'm going down again." He sat on the sled and pushed himself over the hill.

Cam watched him fly down from the corner of his eye as he advanced on Faith. "I see how you are," he murmured. "Ganging up on the old guy."

"Old." She snorted. "Get over yourself." She sidled sideways, ducking under an angled brace for the deck overhead. "That's why you've got teenaged girls oohing and ahhing all over you." She darted to the side, avoiding the snowball he tossed at her.

"Seems to me the only person who hasn't had snow down her back is you." He sidestepped, following her easily even as he scooped up another handful of snow.

"Proving the superiority of the female species," she said blithely, and ducked again, as elusive as a sprite.

He snorted and some part of him gaped at the easy laughter coming out of him.

How long had it been?

"Doesn't mean a thing," he assured. "Except that your time *is* coming."

Her lips twitched. "I think it's time I be going now. I, um, I have things I need to do."

"Things."

"Yes. Things." Her boots brushed through the snow, wisely widening the distance between them. From down the hill, they could hear Erik still whooping and hollering. Her bright gaze slanted, obviously gauging the distance to the deck steps.

"You won't make it," he murmured.

Her eyebrow peaked, Faith clearly taking that as a challenge. "I used to run a Memorial Day marathon every year when I lived in New Mexico."

"Used to."

She lifted her shoulder. "I moved back home."

He thought that was an interesting turn of phrase. Hadn't she considered New Mexico her home? "A marathon is for endurance. Sprinting is for speed."

"I suppose you ran track, too."

"Oh, yeah."

"Any sport you *didn't* participate in?"

"Gymnastics."

"Not macho enough?"

He grunted. "Not flexible enough. Not fast enough for tennis, either."

Her gaze drifted down his body. "Really," she murmured. Then, while he was stomping down hard on the effect of that unexpected look of hers, she launched herself toward the deck stairs.

In two steps, Cam caught her, and they tumbled into the snow bank angling up the wall. He flipped her scarf loose and grabbed a handful of snow, holding it up, threatening.

She tilted her head back, laughing. She tried to grab

his arm with her hands and he shackled her wrists with one hand, pinning them over her head.

"No. Really. Don't," she begged breathlessly.

His gaze caught on her slender throat. The smooth, long grace of it.

He let the snow fall from his hand.

Her lips parted, eyes flaring.

And rather than pushing snow against that long, slender column, he pressed his lips against it, instead.

She tasted as golden as she looked. And he felt the hitch in her breath as she inhaled sharply.

Her captive wrists jerked against his hold, then went still, and he lifted his head.

She stared up at him, her eyes wide. A living, breathing snow angel, with rosy color riding her cheekbones and unmistakable desire turning her eyes mossy green.

He released her, and she slowly lowered her arms. Her gloved fingers flexed against his shoulders, but didn't push him away. Her lips slowly formed his name, soundless.

He lowered his head. Grazed the coolness of her lips with his.

His down vest crinkled softly as she touched his chest. He lifted his head. Stared down at her, need ripping up his spine.

Her pupils dilated. A swallow worked down her lovely, bared throat.

He swore. And slammed his mouth on hers.

She gasped and he swallowed it. He knew he was too rough, tried to temper himself, only to realize she was right there with him, her mouth open, and her tongue tangling as desperately as his.

Then there was nothing but sensation.

The heat of her.

The softness.

The crunch of snow beneath them when her arms twined around his neck and he caught her waist, hauling her hips against his.

He'd never wanted anything in his life as badly as he wanted her.

The realization yanked him back.

He let go of her, and shot to his feet.

She lay there, swollen lips parted, eyes glazed. Her breath was an audible hiss. Her hair was coming loose of her ponytail. Her coat was open, the waist of her sweater pushed up beneath the swell of her breasts, displaying the bandages that had been necessitated by her rescue of his son.

God.

What the hell was he doing?

She slowly drew her sweater down her stomach. Pushed up with one hand until she was sitting in the snow. "Cameron?" Her voice was low. Husky.

Laura's voice had been higher pitched. More...fragile.

Guilt clawed at him, and *still* the want didn't abate. "I'm sorry." His voice was harsh. Flat. "I shouldn't have done that. I'm not interested in—" The lie only went so far.

It didn't matter. His tone had done the job.

"I see." Her chin angled away. She looked down.

Slowly pulled her coat together and adjusted her gloves. "Please tell Erik goodbye for me." Her voice sounded thick. She rolled gracefully to her feet before he could even offer a hand.

He didn't think it was possible to feel lower than he did. Apparently, it was. "Faith—" But he didn't know what to say to her.

So he said nothing.

He just watched her walk away from him.

And still, he wanted her.

"There's an order of baseball gloves in the back that needs to be checked, if you have a chance to get to it."

Tanya's voice sounded harried over the phone and Faith glanced around the interior of Extension Sporting Goods. "There's only been two customers this afternoon," she commented. "I think I'll probably get to the order. Are Monday evenings always this slow?" She was filling in for Tanya only because her friend was home with a sick Toby.

"It'll pick up when baseball season starts. I really appreciate you coming in. Are you sure you didn't have something else to do?"

Faith closed off the image of Cameron standing over her, his regret for touching her nearly flashing neon from his face. "I'm sure. Take care of your son. Everything here will be fine. I'll drop off the day's receipts in the night deposit at the bank on my way home after I close up."

"You're the best."

"That's what I tell all my friends and relations,"

Faith assured dryly and Tanya chuckled as she hung up, as Faith had intended.

She replaced the phone and picked up the towel she'd been using to polish the glass display case that served as the checkout counter. The customer who had been browsing came over with his ski wax selection, and once Faith rang him up and the man left, the store was silent, except for the low music coming from the radio. The Beach Boys singing about California girls.

It was going to be a slow evening, which was unfortunate. Faith had hoped—when she'd offered to help out Tanya—that she'd be kept busy enough to keep what had happened between her and Cameron the other morning *off* her mind.

So much for that.

She went to the back room and began unloading the new shipment, taking extraordinary care to check every label, every detail.

Still, she couldn't get it out of her head. It had been that way all weekend.

The unspeakable feeling of Cam's kiss, followed by him jumping away from her as if he'd found her poisonous.

Even now, humiliation burned inside her. And she hated it just as much now as she had when Jess had found her wanting, too.

She gathered up an armload of baseball mitts and carried them out to the front just as the door jingled.

Cameron and Erik entered.

The mitts tumbled from her arms, spilling over the

countertop and thudding onto the sturdy brown carpet. "Faith!" Erik's face lit up. "I didn't know you'd be here."

That was painfully evident, given Cameron's frozen expression. "I'm friends with Tanya Winters. She owns this place."

"Cool."

Try as she might, she couldn't keep herself from sneaking a look at Cameron. Not that it mattered, since he was most assuredly *not* looking at her.

But Tanya trusted her to fill in for her, and no matter how much she'd have preferred to go hide in the back room, she made herself round the counter and approach them. "Can I help you find something?"

Erik had shrugged out of his parka and shoved it into his dad's hands as he raced across the spacious store toward the display of climbing gear hanging on one wall. "Cool. Can I climb up it?" He pointed at the mock rocks.

Faith shook her head. "Not that one, I'm afraid. It's just for looks."

"He needs a tennis racket." Cameron's voice was abrupt.

Faith lifted her eyebrows. "Tennis?"

"It's for school." Erik's hands were exploring the display. "I gotta play *summer* in the chorus. Dumb, huh?" He hefted up an enormous coil of nylon rope above his head and nearly tipped over.

"Erik." Cameron grabbed the rope with one hand and hooked it back over the heavy-duty hook. "Leave the stuff alone."

"Tennis rackets are in that aisle." Faith pointed toward a rear corner. "Not a very large selection right now, though."

"I'm sure we'll find something." Cameron stepped around her, heading toward the display.

Faith's teeth sank into the inside of her lip, watching. But her thought wouldn't be contained. "Be less expensive to borrow a racket from someone. The school, even."

Cameron slid one of the three racket styles out of the rack. The grip seemed eclipsed by his long fingers. "Erik." He extended the racket to his son.

Erik barely glanced at it. He was still fascinated with the climbing display. "Whatever."

"It's for *your* play, buddy," Cameron reminded.

Erik made a face. Dragged his feet across the carpet and gave the racket a close-up once-over. "It's pink."

"It has a red stripe," Cameron countered.

Erik grimaced. "Da-ad. It's pink!"

"Magenta, actually," Faith put in. She reached carefully past Cameron and pulled down the second style. It was a slightly larger racket. "What about this one?"

Erik's expression looked no happier. "I don't see why I gotta be in a dumb old program, anyhow. Just 'cause I ain't tone-deaf like—"

"Erik," Cameron prompted blandly. "Pick a racket and be done with it."

"It's *yellow,* Dad. I'll look like a geek."

"Well, your only other choice is this one." Cameron pulled out the last style. "And since it has little pink kittens on the grip, I figured you wouldn't be interested."

"Plenty of guys use these two styles, even with the magenta or yellow," Faith said peaceably.

Erik's head lolled back on his neck. He looked as put upon as any person in the history of the world. "Whatever."

Cameron looked like he was gritting his teeth. "Erik." His tone said volumes.

Faith quickly slid the rackets back in place. "I have a black one at home. He could borrow it."

"No, thank you," Cameron said over Erik's suddenly interested "cool."

"Aw, *Dad.*"

"Pick a racket."

The two males looked at each other, clearly in some battle of wills. The best thing for her to do would be to stay out of it. "I really don't mind," she said, proving she had never learned her lesson about doing what was best. "It seems a shame to spend this much on a racket that he's only going to use for one school program. Unless you're planning to learn tennis?"

Erik looked askance.

Cam looked irritated. "You don't have to go out of your way."

She had her own share of irritation rippling down her spine. She eyed him. "Believe me. I won't. If you want the racket, you'll have to come by and pick it up." She waited a beat. "I'll leave it on my front porch for you."

If she'd expected Cameron to be bothered by her dig

at his seeming lack of graciousness, she was wrong. If anything, the man looked as if he'd rather purchase a hundred tennis rackets than avail himself of her simple offer.

"You didn't wanna buy a racket in the first place," Erik said suddenly. His head appeared from the inside of a round rack holding skiwear, then just as quickly disappeared. A moment later, he was crouched down near the floor, looking at a bookcase full of books and local maps.

"It'd just be for the one evening," Cameron said after a moment.

Faith tucked her fingers in the front pockets of her black jeans. "See that it is," she said evenly. "Since the weather is so nice, I figure the town's tennis courts are due to be open any day."

At last, his lips quirked. "You've got a smart mouth on you."

Her shoulder lifted a little. At least he'd stopped looking as if she'd offered to chop off his foot rather than lend his son a tennis racket.

She moved back to the glass checkout counter and found a piece of paper. She scribbled her address on it and handed it to him. "I really will set it out for you, though," she murmured. "Then it won't matter if I'm out on a call or not and you can get it whenever you want."

"My show is tomorrow night." Erik popped up next to her, a thick picture book on bug collecting in his hands. "You wanna come?"

How could anyone not be enamored of this boy? "I can't," she said regretfully. "I already have plans."

"With who?"

"It's none of your business," Cam told Erik. He folded the paper with her address and tucked it in his lapel pocket. "We need to let Ms. Taylor get back to her work."

She was back to *Ms. Taylor.*

Faith stifled a sigh and wished it didn't hurt quite so much. She looked at Erik, deliberately ignoring the fact that Cameron was clearly ready to leave. "I'll be in Bozeman all day tomorrow."

"You won't get back in time?"

She crouched down and shook her head. "I don't think so. I'm sorry." And she was. Surprisingly so. She'd have thought that she'd rather be anywhere else other than an elementary school.

"That's okay," he said after a moment. "Maybe next time."

Her heart squeezed. "Right."

Erik pointed at the climbing display. "Sometime will you teach me how to do that?"

"I'd like that. But if you want to learn climbing *really* well, you should take a class. The guy who teaches it here—Rick—is phenomenal. Much better than I am. The climbing gym is through that door right there." She pointed to the glass doorway on the right side of the store.

"Can I, Dad? Take a class? When is it?"

"Rick comes every other weekend." Faith rose. One glance at Cameron's set expression told her that the boy was doomed to disappointment.

"No," Cameron said evenly. "You climb enough without adding classes in it."

"Da-ad."

"I said no, Erik."

The boy's head fell back and he stomped off around the rack of ski boots.

Faith pressed her hands together. "Rick focuses on safety first, Cameron. Erik could very well benefit from that." She kept her voice low.

"Always so nice when people who *don't* have kids go around passing advice to those who do."

He might as well have slapped her. "Well, pardon me."

He exhaled noisily. "Look. If you want to go to Erik's thing, go. Don't let me stop you. I won't be trying to kiss you or anything."

"Trust me, Cameron—" her voice shook slightly "—I *am* busy. And contrary to the opinion of the female population of Thunder Canyon High School— all who seem to think you hung the moon—not everything is about *you*. You couldn't have made your disinterest in me more plain."

A crash sounded, followed by Erik's plaintive "Oh, man," and Faith darted around the ski boots to find Erik standing on a shelf, shoeboxes tumbled around him.

Cameron swiftly moved past her and swept Erik off the shelf, setting him on the ground. "When I said you climbed enough already, did you think that was an invitation? Do I need to ground you again?"

Erik looked abashed. His chin tucked down into his chest. "No, sir."

Faith gathered up a few boxes and slid them back into place. "Nothing's broken."

"Small mercies." Cameron handed him his coat and pointed to the door. "Move it."

Erik shrugged into his parka. "See ya', Faith."

"See you, Juan."

Erik's lips barely moved into a smile. He pushed out the door, dejection in every movement.

Faith looked at Cameron.

"Sorry about the mess," he said.

"It'll clean up," she said flatly. "You know, maybe if you'd let Erik *do* more of the things he's interested in—like climbing lessons—he wouldn't need to focus his energies on being mischievous. And *no,* I don't need a child of my own to be able to figure that out."

He grabbed the door that Erik had opened before it could swing closed. "When you *do* have a child of your own, then we'll talk." He strode out and the door sighed shut.

Faith closed her eyes.

Then she and Cameron would *never* be talking.

Because having a child of her own was the one thing she would never be able to do.

Chapter Eight

When Faith drove back into Thunder Canyon the following evening from her trip to Bozeman, she could see the line of cars parked up and down the street around the elementary school before she even drove past.

She tapped her thumb on the steering wheel and slowed even more. The parking lot itself looked wall-to-wall with cars. The high windows on the building where the auditorium was located were brightly lit against the night sky.

The building looked welcoming. As if it exuded a physical aura.

Or maybe it was her own longing that was causing the sensation.

She rubbed her forehead. The day had seemed unending with meetings with Jim Shepherd and the rest of the team. Then lunch, celebrating the engagement of Nathan—the youngest of their group. And after that had come Faith's annual doctor's appointment. She'd been poked and prodded and pronounced fit enough—healing scrapes notwithstanding. Nothing had changed since her last visit, a year earlier. Not that she expected otherwise. She'd already been picked apart, medically speaking. There were no surprises left.

She reached the end of the block and braked at the stop sign. There were no oncoming cars, yet she still didn't proceed.

The engine idled. Warm air whispered from the heater vents. Slow, lazy jazz hummed softly from the CD player.

She reached up and nudged the rearview mirror until it was angled enough to see the reflection of the school behind her.

The toot of a horn warned her that another car had pulled up behind her. She hurriedly adjusted her mirror and drove through the empty intersection, letting the impatient car pass her by.

It wasn't all that late. Not even eight o'clock. And the idea of going home to her dark, empty condominium was suddenly more than she could bear.

So she turned her truck around and drove back toward the cheerfully lit, crowded school. She found a parking spot—well, made herself one at any rate—beneath a streetlight, and strode quickly to the auditorium. She could hear the high pip of youthful voices even before she quietly slipped into the rear of the room.

Folding chairs were set up in neat rows, filling nearly all of the floor space. The children stood on risers on the low stage at one end of the room.

A quartet stood in front of the chorus, Erik among them. A little blond girl about his size was singing a solo at the moment. She was dressed in skiwear and her voice shook a little as she sang about the beauty of winter. Then she took a step back while parental applause rocked the house, and another girl took her place, this one decked out like spring flowers. Faith stepped a little closer, still keeping well to the shadows in the rear of the room. She wasn't altogether surprised to see how Erik stood so still and serious while "Spring" sang her solo. Even though the boy was an utter ball of energy, she knew he was perfectly capable of focusing it when he chose. She'd experienced it herself when he'd pitted his prowess at checkers against her.

She didn't realize that her gaze was methodically working along the rows of chairs until it stopped.

Cameron sat in the third row from the front. Dead center.

And he held a small video recorder in his hand.

It wasn't as if he were the only parent present capturing the event on video. From where she stood, she could see dozens of faintly lit video camera screens in varying sizes. But the sight of Cameron—

She blew out a soft breath, and tugged nervously at her ponytail.

The sight of Cameron taping his son definitely did something to her insides. And it didn't matter at all that inside her head, she could still hear his words to her the previous night.

And even though *that* should have been warning enough, she stayed there, rapt, through the rest of the performance, only managing to drag her attention from Cameron when Erik stepped forward for his solo.

His voice shook a little, just as the others had, but with each stanza, he gained confidence, until he was belting out his lines, and by the time he and the other soloists stepped back into their spots on the risers, the audience was practically cheering. The children's smiles beamed out, and along with everyone else, Faith clapped until her palms ached when the performance ended a few songs later.

She fully intended to disappear again before Erik saw her, but that plan was foiled when the parents made beelines for the door the moment the rest of the lights came up. Unprepared for the mass exodus, Faith found herself stuck behind the row of chairs.

Cameron spotted her first.

His footsteps didn't falter, but even across the distance of a dozen rows of chairs, she felt the sharpness of his gaze fastening on her face.

He'd tasted of coffee.

Her face heated. She looped her long scarf around her neck, which regrettably only made her feel warmer. But she refused to fidget. Particularly when he was watching her so steadily, and providing no hint whatsoever as to what his thoughts were.

While hers, on the other hand, kept running down the same paths until they'd made deep enough ruts that she could have sailed a ship in them.

What was she doing here?

Was it Erik that drew her, or Erik's dad?

Or both?

Did it even matter? The sly whisper worked through her, ringing in her thoughts as Cameron stopped a foot away from her. His big hand eclipsed the camera he held, and the child's backpack—probably fat with books and goodness knew what else—slung over one shoulder looked rather minuscule.

His jaw was blurred by a five o'clock shadow, but she could still see the muscle ticking there.

And everything female inside her went foolishly soft.

"Thought you were busy," he said after a moment. He took another step forward to allow a woman with a stroller to get past them.

"I was. I finished."

His lids drooped and her lips suddenly tingled. She pulled off her scarf. "Erik's quite the performer," she said cautiously. She didn't want a repeat of the previous night.

He nodded slowly. "Just give him an audience."

Her hands bunched the scarf. "When I was his age I could never have done a solo like that." She swallowed. "Well, I couldn't do it *now* for that matter."

His lips tilted slightly. "His mother liked an audience, too." Apparently, Cameron didn't want to have an argument, either.

"And...you?"

"I prefer a more private production."

She nearly choked and whipped the scarf back around her neck. She was so far out of her element it was a wonder she wasn't drowning in her own rutted thoughts.

She simply could not figure the man out, and it was better if she'd stop trying.

"I, um, I should be going. Tell Erik I thought he was great."

"Tell him yourself." His gaze skipped past her and he lifted his chin a little.

Faith turned to see Erik coming into the auditorium from the entrance. Two little girls, the soloists, were hard on his heels.

"Hey, Faith." Erik grinned, but seemed to take her presence without surprise. As if he'd half expected her to show up no matter what she'd said to the contrary.

Since she *was* there, perhaps Erik was on to something.

"You and Dad gotta come to our classroom now," he said blithely. "You gotta see our *work.* We been pinning it up on the bulletin boards for a whole week."

Faith's gaze darted up to Cameron's. "Oh, I really should get home." Her voice strangled when Cameron closed his hand over her elbow.

"Lead the way," he told his son.

"She's the lady who rescued you, huh," Spring whispered not so quietly to Erik, casting a curious look up at Faith.

"Uh-huh."

The other girl wasn't so shy. She tilted her blond head and addressed Faith directly. "Do you get to keep the gold you found?"

Faith's eyebrows shot up. "Only gold *I* found in the mine was named Erik. It's been other people who are catching gold fever, I think."

The boy rolled his eyes, but giggled a little as the kids scurried ahead. "Hurry up, Dad. Or there's not gonna be any cookies left by the time we get there."

Faith still hung back when Cameron started to follow. "I really should go."

"Go where?"

Through her long-sleeved sweater, she felt his thumb smooth over her elbow.

An empty home? An elementary school packed with lively children?

Both caused their share of pain.

"Faith?"

She swallowed, knowing her hesitation went on too long. Too obvious, yet unable to do one single thing about it now. The man's kiss had hinted at heaven, all wrapped up in sinful temptation. But he'd pushed her away as if she'd turned vile. And now…now she didn't know what he was doing.

Or what she was doing there.

It all came back to that.

And for some reason, it made her want to sit down and cry. But she hadn't cried in a very, very long time. And she'd be darned if she'd start now.

"Maybe for a few minutes," she said finally.

He nodded, not smiling. "Erik'll be pleased."

"And you?" The words were out before she could think twice. His eyes narrowed a fraction. And she quickly waved her hand. "Never mind. Probably better if we leave that one alone." Proving that cowardice was alive and well and dwelling inside her, she hurriedly turned and followed after Erik.

The classroom, when they got there, seemed packed with people. But like a determined fish, Erik wriggled between them and latched onto Faith's hand the moment she stepped through the doorway. She didn't have to look back to see if Cameron was there. She could feel him in the sparks of energy tickling her spine even when he was yards behind her.

"Come and see my desk." Erik tugged at her as he dove back into the fray.

There was little Faith could do but follow. She admired his desk and the neat journal that was taped to the top surface. When he lifted the lid, she was suitably impressed with the order of his supplies inside.

"We all hadda clean our desks during class today," he admitted, grinning. "I had a whole bag of trash."

Cameron's hand closed over the back of her neck as he leaned over them both, looking at the desk as well.

How was it possible to freeze and melt all at the same time?

Yet that's exactly how she felt.

She stared blindly at a vocabulary workbook and tried to pretend there was nothing more extraordinary going on than Erik's pencils being lined up like a half-dozen dutiful soldiers.

Fortunately, Erik's teacher was trying to call order to the group.

"Sit here," Erik hissed and pushed her to his undersize chair.

Faith sat, which was good since her legs felt oddly insubstantial. Once the room was more or less quiet, the teacher—a humorous, middle-aged woman whom Faith had never met—welcomed the parents, and briefly outlined the work the students had been doing for the past semester. She pointed out the various projects that were displayed around the room, and then invited everyone to continue drinking punch and eating the cookies.

Erik, along with a dozen other seven-year-olds, darted toward the refreshments that were set up on a short table beneath the blackboard. He was back before Faith could even start to make noises about leaving again, bearing a napkin loaded with several cookies. He dumped it on her lap, then was off again.

Faith looked up at Cameron, half afraid that she'd find him looking at her and wishing it were his beloved wife sitting there, instead. But his eyes were only amused as he leaned over and plucked a chocolate-chip cookie from her lap. "Have a cookie," he said blandly.

Erik had left them with at least a half-dozen of them, and Faith found herself smiling, too.

"Does he like cookies?"

"Don't all seven-year-old boys?"

She watched Cameron finish off his cookie in two bites. "Don't all grown men?"

"We never had homemade cookies when I was growing up," he said. He dumped Erik's backpack on the floor near her feet, set the video camera on the desk, and hunkered down on his heels next to her chair. He studied the selection remaining, then reached. His knuckle brushed her knee as he picked up a sugar cookie sprinkled with red crystalline sugar.

Sheer effort kept her from shifting in the chair. "Why not? Your mom didn't bake?"

"I doubt my mother even knows how to turn on an oven," he said dryly. "Might mess up her hundred-dollar manicure."

"Your parents are wealthy?"

"Oh, yeah." He finished the cookie. Brushed the crumbs from his fingertip on his thigh.

A muscular thigh that looked hard and solid as it bulged against his well-cut charcoal gray trousers.

She quickly looked back at the napkin and cookies in her own lap.

"We had cookies, of course. Beautifully prepared by Denver's finest pastry chefs." He shifted a little, putting one arm behind her on the back of the chair.

She was finding it difficult to breathe. She'd spent many an afternoon in the kitchen with her mom and sisters baking cookies. For holidays. For fun. "My parents live in Arizona," she announced baldly.

"Were you close to them?"

She nodded. "Still are. They still hold hands. It's great." An enduring marriage like her parents' is what she'd thought she'd have when she'd said her vows to Jess.

So much for that.

"Any other siblings beside the doc?"

"Sisters. Both younger." She picked up a cookie. Nibbled a corner of it. Oatmeal raisin.

Figures. She loathed oatmeal raisin. That's what she got for letting herself be so distracted by a man. By *Cameron*.

"How long were you married?"

She started. "Six years. You?"

"Five. You still love him?"

Her fingers went lax and the cookie tumbled to the sturdy green-flecked carpet. "That's a very personal question."

"Yeah." His head nearly brushed her thigh as he leaned over and retrieved the cookie. He set it on the corner of the desk and looked back at her. "Are you?"

"No." She'd called Erik a jumping bean, but it was *her* nerves that were jumping all over the place now. "Are you?" she challenged.

"In love with your ex? Not likely."

Her lips pressed together. "Ha-ha."

His gaze was on the cookies again. "Yes."

Her jumping nerves collided and collapsed into wreckage. Well. She'd asked, hadn't she? "I'm sorry."

His gaze slanted to her face. "For what?"

"I don't know."

He slowly took another cookie. "This is what Laura wanted," he said after a moment.

"Broken gingerbread?"

His lips twisted. "A regular life like this." He lifted his chin, encompassing the families who milled around the room. The children who raced back and forth. "She wanted to move here so damned bad. Had a vision in her head of the kind of childhood Erik would have. The kind of home we'd have. How we'd be part of the whole small-town deal."

She could see each individual lash of his thick, sooty eyelashes. Could see the fine lines barely webbing out from the corners of his dark eyes. "Then she'd be pleased," Faith said quietly. "That you have what she'd wanted for you."

"Yeah." His gaze roved over the room and she could practically feel the restlessness seeping out of his pores. "Too late, though," he added grimly.

She curled her fingers, realizing that she'd actually begun lifting her hand as if to touch his hair. And wouldn't that be the height of folly? "Because she… died."

"Because I didn't start living the life she wanted until *after* she died." He pushed to his feet. "Don't think Erik's coming with punch anytime soon. I'll be back." He headed toward the line of people at the refreshment table.

Faith watched him go. He wasn't necessarily the tallest, or even the biggest man there. He did have height and mile-wide shoulders on his side, true. But the thing about Cameron that made him stand out from the others was not his physicality. It was something…deeper. Something that came up from his soul.

And rather than being put off by his confirmation that he still loved his wife, she feared she was only more intrigued than ever.

Realizing she was staring—and probably drooling on herself as well—she looked down at Erik's journal. It was displayed in a manner clearly meant to be read, so she flipped open the thick paper that served as the cover, and looked at the first page. Erik's writing was slapdash, as if he could hardly be bothered with penmanship when there were more interesting things in the world to attend to. But it improved as she paged through, reading the weekly entries that covered a span of about three months.

At the end was his recounting of his adventure down the mine shaft. He'd even drawn a picture—a well-drawn picture for that matter—of himself, being drawn up the shaft by the safety harness and rope, with Faith down below him.

"He inherited his mother's ability to draw, too."

She looked up, already aware of Cameron's presence before he'd spoken. He held out a clear plastic cup filled with red punch. She took it, carefully avoiding his long fingers, and sipped. "You don't draw?"

"Stick figures are more my speed," he assured dryly. "Toss in a little calculus, trig and math analysis, and that's my art."

"And high school sports."

"Yeah." He drank from his own cup. "I think Erik's permanently camped out at the refreshment table. He doesn't usually get homemade cookies, either."

"Maybe I'll have to get out my cookie sheets," she murmured.

"You bake?"

"I'm not all about the search and rescue," she said dryly.

His lashes dropped. "Yeah. I know. I need to apologize. For last night."

At least he hadn't apologized for the kiss.

Again.

She wasn't sure she'd have been able to take it, if he had. "We both said things we probably shouldn't have."

His index finger tapped his plastic cup. "Truth is, you'll make a great mom. When you decide to have a family." He looked around the room. "There are at least six people here who don't have the interest in their own child that you have in Erik. Who would rather be anywhere other than here."

Faith was grateful his attention was elsewhere. She choked down her punch in a huge gulp, then transferred the napkin and remains of the cookies to the desktop and stood. "I don't suppose school functions are everyone's cup of tea."

"They weren't my parents'." His voice was matter-of-fact. "Only time they came was when it was time to pick me up from boarding school at the end of each term."

She tugged her scarf back into place and picked up her coat. He'd gone to a boarding school? Sounded lonely.

"I have to go," she said. "I'll just sneak by and tell Erik. If I can get his attention away from his girlfriends there."

"*Girl*friends?" His head snapped around.

There was nothing blasé in his expression now. And if Faith weren't feeling so off-kilter, she might have found his surprise amusing. "Also known as Winter and Spring. They've barely let him out of their sight since we came in the classroom." She headed toward the refreshment table and worked her way toward Erik.

"Can we go tobogganing again soon?" he asked after she'd told him it was time for her to leave.

"Depends on my schedule," she said honestly. He had a smear of chocolate on his chin and the front of his hair stood up in a cowlick.

Her head told her she would be better off staying far, far away from either of the Stevensons.

But her heart?

She tweaked Erik's tumbled hair and crouched down to his level. "I'll see what I can arrange, okay?"

"Cool." He smiled. And even though he was surrounded by classmates, he leaned forward. His hug was brief, but tight.

And it stole her heart.

She rose and turned. Felt the slam of Cameron's brown gaze when she saw him standing just behind them, and had to look down, unable to withstand the intensity of it.

"I'll walk you to your car," he told her. "Erik, you stay in this classroom until I get back."

Erik looked surprised. But he nodded. "'Bye, Faith."

She winked, though what she wanted to do was hug the boy again. "'Bye, Juan."

"How come she calls you Juan?" she heard Spring whisper as she and Cameron headed toward the door. Before they left the building, she stopped to pull on her coat. Cameron took it from her and held it up for her.

She tucked her tongue between her teeth and silently slid her arms into the sleeves. Then he closed his hands over her shoulders and turned her to face him. His fingers brushed her chin when he buttoned it.

"Faith! Wait!"

She drew in an unsteady breath and looked back to see Erik racing down the hall.

"Erik, I told you to wait in the classroom."

"I know, Dad. But I forgot this." He pushed an over-size sheet of paper at Faith. "I made this for you. I had to get it down off the bulletin board."

Faith took the paper and turned it until she could see the front. It was a watercolor painting and the sturdy brick lines of the fire station were clearly recognizable.

"That's you," he stabbed his finger at the slightly blurry figure astride a snowmobile outside the building.

"I figured." She couldn't stand it. She leaned down and kissed his forehead. "Thank you. I'm going to hang it up at home when I get there."

He rolled his eyes a little, but grinned, then he was racing back down the hallway toward his classroom.

"Yeah," Cameron murmured. "You'll be a great mom." His hand touched the small of her back even as he reached forward to push open the heavy door.

Cold air washed over her hot face as she stepped outside. "Actually," her fingers tightened unconsciously on the corner of Erik's painting. "I really don't plan to have kids."

She felt his sidelong look at that and quickened her step. Cameron's long legs easily kept pace, however. And when they reached her SUV, he snorted softly. "Think making your own parking space where there is none might just be worse than double-parking."

"There's a foot of snow between my wheels and the grass," she defended lightly. "I'm not damaging anything. And the only one who'd delight in giving me another ticket would be Bobby Romano."

"*Another* ticket. Wild woman." He pulled open the driver's side door. "You didn't lock it."

"Not much point." She'd never been called a wild woman before. She thought she might just like it. "Thunder Canyon isn't a hotbed of criminal activity." She climbed up into the vehicle.

He stepped closer, inside the open door. "Maybe not. But it'd be safer for you."

"I think I'm pretty safe," she demurred.

The streetlight overhead shined down on his bare head, casting his dark auburn head with a gilded sheen. He stood close enough that she could feel the warmth of him. His coat hung open, and it would only take one small move and she could slide her hand over the pale gray shirt that draped his hard chest.

"Are you?"

Her lips were tingling again. "Hmm?"

His deep voice seemed to drop even more. "Safe."

She curled her hand tightly around the steering wheel. A much *safer* alternative than touching him. The only one in danger of anything was her. But maybe it was better that Cameron was still in love with his wife. There was no danger of her being hurt again, the way she had been when Jess walked out, if Cameron found out just how much she was lacking.

"I'm safe as houses," she finally whispered.

He leaned down, his mouth hovering inches above hers.

A car drove by, tooting its horn. "Hey, Coach! G'luck on Friday!"

Cameron straightened. He lifted his hand in acknowledgment of the drive-by well-wisher. "Parking under a streetlight." His voice was dry. "Perfect."

She stuck the key in the ignition, rather amazed that she managed it on the first try. "It's *safer*," she said.

He was silent for a long heartbeat. Then he smiled. He backed up, out of the way of the door. "Drive carefully."

"Always."

But he wasn't so breezy. "I mean it, Faith. Be careful."

She nodded slowly. "I'll be careful, Cameron."

He studied her for a moment longer then, apparently satisfied, he nodded once and pushed her door closed. He stepped away from the truck so she'd have room to back out of her impromptu parking slot.

She drove away, with the reflection of him in her rearview mirror.

He stood there until she turned out of sight and she continued on home.

Safe?

Who was she kidding?

Chapter Nine

"We forgot to get your tennis racket back to you last night."

Faith's hand tightened around the telephone and she managed to scatter the pages of the budget she'd been working on for Jim across her desk.

The last voice she'd expected to hear on the other end of the phone when it rang was Cameron's.

"And here I was about to put in a missing racket report." Her voice was deliberately light.

"I still owe you a dinner."

"You don't *owe* me anything."

"You didn't have a chance to eat last Friday at The Hitching Post. I'm tossing some steaks on the grill tonight. If you're interested."

She *was* interested. That was the problem.

"Erik's been practicing with the toboggan, too. Think he has some trick he wants to show you."

She pressed her fingertips against her forehead. Shifts had just changed and there was a lot of commotion inside the station. "I'll be on call this evening. I wouldn't want to disappoint Erik if I get called out."

"He'd just have something new to brag about at school tomorrow."

In his background, she could hear a school bell. It sounded even noisier on his end than it did at the fire station. And it took no effort at all on her part to envision Cameron at his desk, students pouring into his classroom. "Cameron—"

"Erik's not the only one who'd like you to come."

She swallowed. Hard.

"You still there?"

"Yes." She pushed out the word. "All right. Um… can I bring anything?"

"Just yourself. Come by around seven. We've got a practice game after school. *Romance*," his voice sharpened. "If you want to avoid the principal's office, get off the desk." His tone changed again. "See you tonight."

"Okay." She'd barely gotten the word out when he'd hung up, and she sat there for a long moment staring at the receiver in her hand.

"Works better when you talk *into* it, Blondie." Derek stopped by her desk. He dropped a plastic container by her elbow. "Cake."

She finally hung up the telephone. Glanced at the

container. "Thanks." She shifted it to the side, off the budget papers.

His eyebrows shot up. "Okay. Tanya was right. Something's up with you."

"Nothing's up with me."

He leaned way over, crossing his arms on the desk, to peer into her face. "That's chocolate cake in there, and you're *not* diving into it? Something is up all right. Wanna tell Uncle Derek about it?"

She rolled her eyes. "Don't be ridiculous."

"Have anything to do with the coach?"

Faith's cheeks warmed. "No."

"Even though he was kissing you last night at the elementary school?"

She gaped. "How…he was not." He hadn't kissed her, because of the car that had driven by.

Derek was grinning, looking knowing. Faith bunched up the papers and tapped them against the desk, squaring the edges. "He's just still feeling grateful."

"Keep telling yourself that, Blondie." He nudged the container. "Better eat this up before word gets out that I didn't bring anyone else any dessert. You might find yourself in a dogfight or something."

She snatched the container, protective, and tucked it in her desk drawer. "Nobody gets between me and chocolate," she assured him.

But Faith didn't get a chance to eat the chocolate cake that afternoon. Nor did she make it to Cameron's for dinner.

The entire team was called out just after noon, when an AMBER alert was issued for a three-year-old girl who'd gone missing just outside of Bozeman.

And it was well after midnight when she finally dragged herself home, where the only thing to welcome her was the flashing red light on her answering machine. She hit the Play button on her way into the kitchen.

Her mother's voice trilled out, talking about the beautiful weather they were having in Arizona, and when was Faith going to take a vacation and come see them?

Faith opened the refrigerator door. Stared at the unexciting contents. Derek's chocolate masterpiece was still tucked away in her desk drawer at work. She closed the door and leaned wearily back against it. Listened to her brother's message, calling to see if she wanted to have lunch later that week. Then a third call.

Cameron.

She pushed herself away from the refrigerator and left the kitchen to eye the message machine, which sat next to the phone on a small maple telephone stand that her mom had passed on to her years earlier. She pressed the Stop button. Rewound it a few seconds. Pressed Play.

Faith. This is Cam. Practice ran late. But you're not here, anyway. Heard the AMBER alert on the radio. Figured you're out on it. Guess I'll have to feed you another time.

She crossed her arms, avoiding the temptation to rewind the message and listen to it again.

But the messages weren't finished.

Faith. Cam. It's after eleven. Just saw the news. Call me when you get in. I don't care how late. Call. He reeled off the number.

The machine's red light stopped flashing. All of the new messages had been played.

She unfolded her arms, feeling just tired and weak enough to actually dial that number. But something held her back. Cowardice? Sensibility?

She went into her bedroom and replaced the uniform she'd been wearing for so many hours with her thick, comfortable robe. She pulled off the clasp holding back her ponytail, and dropped the gold loop on her dresser, rubbing her hand against her tired scalp.

The phone rang, sounding sharp and imperious. And she knew, just glancing at the extension, who would be calling her at this hour.

She sat on the side of the bed and slowly picked it up. "Hello?"

"You didn't call." Cameron's voice was low. Deep.

A frisson rippled through her. "I just got in a few minutes ago. I'm sorry. I didn't get a chance to call you before dinner. We were pretty busy."

"Are you okay?"

She reached out for a pillow and pulled it over her lap. "It was a...tough night." Her throat felt tight. "You saw the news?"

"Yeah."

So he knew the child had been found too late. Three tiny years of innocence obliterated in an instant because of one man's malevolent insanity.

"Have you had to deal with other cases like this?"

Where a child was killed by an abductor? "No. We've had more than a few that ended up being a recovery rather than rescue." And it never got any easier. "But nothing like this." Accidents versus heinous intention. "The FBI was there. Police crawling all over the place. Local, county, state. Must've been around seventy-five searchers." Her eyes ached, dry and so tired. "It was…awful, Cameron. We found her poor little body stuck under a bush near a highway rest stop."

"Where were you?"

She pinched her eyes closed. "On the other side of the highway. A witness had called in a report of a driver pitching something out their car window—a car similar in description to one used by the suspected abductor—in that area. We were in tight critical spacing. Nathan—he's the youngest SAR—found the body. He's pretty wrecked."

"Jesus."

She wished she could get the image out of her head. "I'm sorry I didn't call and cancel dinner."

He made a rough noise. "Come on, Faith. Do you think that really matters?"

"It always had to Jess." She hadn't meant to admit that.

"Your ex? He was a firefighter, wasn't he?"

"Yes." She didn't recall ever telling him that fact.

"You'd think he'd have had a better grasp on priorities."

Faith carefully exhaled. "He didn't figure I needed to be out saving anything when he was already doing it himself." No. Jess had wanted her home having his babies. And when she'd failed in that regard, he'd traded her in for a better model.

"Do you want me to come over?"

Forget carefully exhaling. She felt as if her breath were knocked right out of her. "Why?" she croaked.

"Because you've had a tough night. You shouldn't be alone."

She rubbed her eyes a little harder. "You can't leave Erik alone. Particularly at this hour."

"Then call someone. Your brother. Or your friend who owns the sporting goods store. Tanya, right?"

It undid her that he recalled such specifics. "Chris is undoubtedly on duty, and if he's not, he's grabbing what little sleep he manages to get between the hospital and the ranch. And Tanya's still dealing with Toby, her son. He's had the flu for the past few days." She opened her eyes, but the image of that poor toddler seemed seared into her brain, overriding the pale, sage green bedroom wall she'd painted just a few months earlier. "I appreciate the concern. But I'm fine."

He made a soft, disbelieving sound. "Right."

Her spine stiffened a little. "I'm not some fragile thing, Cameron."

"No. You're human," he countered evenly. "And this has nothing to do with your competence or abilities. Which, frankly, might intimidate the hell out of some people."

"But not you?" Some portion of her mind realized that she was shaking. "Never mind. I didn't mean that."

"You make me feel a lot of things, Faith. Intimidated isn't one of them."

Her eyes stung unmercifully. "Cameron—"

He swore softly. "What the hell are we doing here, Faith?"

She trembled harder. "I don't know. I, um, I'm going to take a shower." Maybe she'd be able to warm up, then. "And go to bed. Where you should be. You have school tomorrow." The clock face mocked her. "Today," she amended.

"Faith—"

"I'm *fine*," she spoke quickly, over him. "Good night, Cameron." She quickly leaned over and hung up the phone.

Then she stayed there, hunched over the pillow bunched against her abdomen. But he didn't call back.

And after several minutes of silence, she finally stopped expecting the phone to ring again. She went into her bathroom and took her shower, just as she'd said she was going to do. And even though the room was dripping with steam when she finally stepped out a long while later, she still felt cold inside.

She pulled on an ancient pair of sweats, wrapped herself in her thick robe for good measure, and went back into the living room. She flipped on the television. But the only things on were an infomercial touting the miraculous effects of a hair tonic and all-night news.

She wasn't up to seeing a news report of that night's horror so she settled for the infomercial, even though she didn't think she was going bald anytime soon. But the low noise was better than silence and she went into the kitchen. She hadn't eaten since breakfast and her stomach was protesting, but the thought of food was more than she could stand. She eyed the bottle of wine Tanya had brought over when they'd had dinner together last week. But when she reached into the refrigerator, she pulled out the jug of milk instead.

Hot chocolate was a better choice.

She pulled out a saucepan, sloshed milk into it and stuck it on the stove to heat.

Her head was pounding.

In a bowl, she mixed up real cocoa with sugar, a dash of salt and a splash of vanilla, the way her mom had always done when she was little.

The bottle of aspirin sitting on the kitchen table was empty. Her silent reminder to buy another when she managed to get herself to the store. Fortunately, she had a stash in her first-aid kit in the SUV. She turned down the heat under the milk, pushed her feet into the fur-lined boots sitting by the door and went outside to retrieve it.

She found the bottle just where it was supposed to be, and shook out a few pills into her palm. Cold night air whisked over her wet head so she hurriedly locked up the SUV again and turned back to the sidewalk.

Cameron stood in her path.

She swayed. God. Now she was seeing him in her mind, too.

Only hallucinations didn't reach out and grab your elbows with strong, remarkably gentle hands.

Did they?

"What the hell are you doing out here?" His voice was rough.

She opened her palm. "Aspirin."

He exhaled noisily, and closed his arm over her shoulder. "Let's get you inside. You don't even have on a coat."

She found herself hustled up the walk. She wasn't sure he hadn't just lifted her right off her feet, when it came down to it. And she was still staring at him when he let go of her to close her front door.

He set the tennis racket he'd been holding in one hand on the narrow table by the door where she always dropped her keys and mail, and shrugged off his shearling coat, which he dumped over the top of her weighted-down coat tree. "What do I smell?"

As if he'd been there a dozen times, he walked right past her into her small kitchen. She followed, seeing him pull the saucepan off the heat in just enough time to keep it from bubbling over. He turned the heat off.

In her preoccupation, she hadn't turned the heat down. She'd turned it too high.

"What are you doing here? Where's Erik?"

He opened one cupboard. Then another. Found a glass that he filled with water and handed it to her.

She stupidly remembered the aspirin in her hand, and swallowed it quickly. Then he took the glass back and set it in her sink.

"Erik's still asleep in his bed at home," he finally answered, apparently satisfied now that she'd swallowed her aspirin. "Todd Gilmore came over to stay with him."

"Todd Gilmore. As in your student, Todd."

"Yeah. He watches Erik now and then for me."

"In the middle of the night?"

"No. This is a first. Gilmore's a night owl, though. Brags about it every day when he's falling asleep in my second-hour math class. I knew he'd still be up when I called him, and he was. Plus, he lives in the house next door to me," he reminded her.

She could feel her face heating under the steady weight of his gaze. "Does he know you were coming over here?"

"He knows."

"Great." She could just imagine the gossip that would fly now. "I told you I was fine, Cameron. I don't need your…coddling."

He was standing with his back to her stove, a good ten feet from her. "What *do* you need, Faith?"

She stared at him, mute, while too many things tangled inside her head, her chest, to be let free.

He made a rough sound, and crossed the kitchen in two strides. "Think you may be a harder case than I am," he muttered, and pulled her against him, tucking her head against his chest.

She shuddered. His warmth, his strength, his… *comfort*…nearly more than she could bear. "Cameron." She didn't know what else to say.

He just held her.

And a tear leaked down her cheek. She rubbed her cheek against his soft beige shirt. His fingers slowly threaded through her hair. And another tear fell.

"I don't even know if they've caught the guy," she murmured at last.

"They did. News was full of it." His lips pressed against the top of her head. Her forehead. Then he cupped her face and tilted it back to his gaze. His thumb slowly brushed over her damp cheek.

"I hope they hang him," she said thickly.

His palms were warm on her face. And there was no judgment in his dark gaze. He just slowly tucked her back against his chest, rocking ever so slightly. "How'd you ever end up in search and rescue?"

She curled her hands over his biceps and closed her eyes. "Because of Jess," she admitted. "My ex-husband." She was silent for a long moment, soaking in the warmth of Cameron's body through her completely unappealing robe and sweats. "I was actually going for a teaching degree."

"In?"

"Elementary education." She sighed when his fingers started threading through her hair again then rubbed gently against her scalp.

"Then what?"

She lowered her head a little when his fingers found her nape and massaged there. Heaven. "Jess was with the fire department already. We were out on a departmental picnic and a child got separated from his folks." She sighed, angling her head a little more. Oh, he was good at that. "I'd always been into outdoor activities. Camping. Sports. It's one of the things Jess and I had in common." Things that hadn't been enough to hold them together. "After that picnic…I don't know. I saw what SAR was all about, up close and personal. I changed course a little."

"Was the kid found?"

She nodded. "Safe and sound and sunburned as all get-out."

"Were you and Jess already married?"

"About six months by then." No matter how good Cameron's hands felt on her, she didn't particularly want to discuss her marriage. She shifted, lifting her head and his hands fell away, but only to transfer to her shoulders.

Where he found a whole new set of tired muscles.

She closed her eyes, her lips curving despite herself. "You could have a second career," she murmured after a moment. "Cameron Stevenson. Master masseur."

"Third career."

"Right." Her head had found its way back to his chest. "What was it you did in Denver?"

"Made rich people richer." His palms slid beneath the robe and the soft, worn terry cloth slid off her shoulders. It bunched loosely around her waist, still held in place by the tie. The collar of her faded gray sweatshirt had long been cut out and his fingers slid beneath it, finding the bare skin of her shoulders.

Her hands slid down his sides, finding purchase in the empty belt loops of his blue jeans. "And you, too?"

"And me." His voice dropped even lower.

"So, you, um…" She hesitated, then let out a long sigh when his fingertips pressed firmly against her back. He'd reached up beneath her sweatshirt, she realized dimly.

"I…what?"

The robe's tie finally gave up the ghost and the once-pink terry cloth slid to her feet. His fingers swept down her spine. Found the ache at the small of her back even through the worn-thin fabric of her sweat-pants.

What had she been going to say? "Ah…right. Didn't go into teaching to make your fortune."

He laughed softly. "Who does?"

She wasn't cold anymore. She was melting. From the inside out. "But you changed…oh, that feels good…your, um, mind about making rich people richer?"

"Mmm-hmm."

"Why?"

His fingers hesitated for a moment and she held her breath, yearning for him not to stop.

His fingers pressed again, moving in a tight circle right above her rear, and she let out an appreciative sigh.

"I had more degrees than anyone could ever need," he murmured. "And a client list longer than my arm. I couldn't keep up with them from here—not when they were spread out all over the states. I was travel-ing all the time. Gone more than I was here. And after Laura…died—" he exhaled "—not working wasn't an option. I had to find something to do. And it wasn't hard to add a teaching certificate to my other creden-tials."

He hadn't turned to teaching until after his wife had passed away. Her hands slid up his torso, exploring the hard ridges of muscle and sinew. "How did she die?"

For a long moment she feared he wouldn't answer.

His head brushed hers. His mouth touched her shoulder and she felt his lips moving against her skin. "She was out antique hunting. It was raining. Her SUV hydroplaned into a tree. She never had a chance."

Her hands slid behind him.

"She was always on me about traveling too much. Was afraid with all the flying I was doing that something would happen." He sighed again. "And she was the one who—" His voice broke off and he lifted his head. His eyes were shadowed. "She wasn't even fifty miles away from Thunder Canyon. Erik was with her."

She sucked in a hard breath. "Oh, Cam."

"He was belted in his safety seat. Laura had always been rabid about that."

And ever since, he'd been afraid of losing his son, too. No wonder the man was so protective where Erik was concerned.

"I didn't give her what she wanted while she was alive. So I'm doing it now," he said gruffly. His hands lowered to his sides and he stepped back. "Living the life she'd wanted."

She frowned a little. "And what about what you want?"

He was backing up. Until he planted his hands on the kitchen counter on either side of him. "It doesn't matter what I want. This is what I'm doing."

She looked at the floor tiles, measuring them off between her feet and his. He couldn't put more distance between them unless he left the room. "Which doesn't include doing this," she concluded. Her voice was barely audible. "Doing...me."

"Don't." In contrast to hers, his voice was sharp. Harsh. "Don't reduce this."

She pressed her lips together for a long moment, until she felt vaguely certain that her vocal chords might work. "Have you—" Did she even want to know the answer to this? "Have you been with...anyone since she died?"

His fingertips were pressing so hard against the countertop that they looked white.

And she chickened out. "I'm sorry. It's none of my business." She of all people should know there were some things too private for discussion.

His lips twisted. "If not your business, then whose?"

Which she didn't know how to take. "I don't know what you want from me." She swallowed, and tugged the sagging collar of her sweatshirt back up her shoulder. She had to look a fright.

But his gaze, when it ran over her, told her differently.

A fact that only added to the confusion mired inside of her.

"I want to know that you're all right," he said after a moment. "I *need* to know that."

Her heart squeezed. "Why?"

He just eyed her. "I don't know."

She absorbed that. "I'm...tired." To-the-bone tired. She bent down and picked up her robe, pulling it securely around her shoulders. "I'm going to bed. I'm fine. And you can lock the door on your way out."

Chapter Ten

"And you're telling me that Cameron came over just to make sure you were okay after the search, and then *left* without…?" Tanya's head was close to Faith's, her voice barely a whisper.

Faith dabbed the end of her French fry into the puddle of ketchup on the side of her plate. "He just came to make sure I was okay," she said evenly. There were four other women seated around the table at The Hitching Post that Saturday afternoon. They were there for their official no-hearts Valentine's Day lunch.

Tanya had been included only because her husband was still on duty at the station. *She* wasn't officially manless, as the rest were.

Frannie Waters, Becka Townsend, Sharona Miles

and Diana Crocker had all graduated from high school the same year as Faith and Tanya. Ever since, every Valentine's Day, those without significant others had gotten together for lunch. Not a single year had passed without at least two of them meeting.

"My soon-to-be-ex golfs with Theo Gilmore," Frannie said. Her hand was wrapped firmly around a strawberry daiquiri. Her second, and she vowed it would be her last for the day. "And he told me—as he was dropping off our final papers, mind you—that the coach called Todd over to watch that little hooligan after *midnight.*"

"Erik isn't a hooligan," Faith defended, only to wish she'd kept her mouth shut when she saw Frannie elbow Diana, knowingly. That was the problem with old high school friends. They never forgot how to push your buttons.

"Told you she liked the coach," Frannie singsonged.

"What does it matter," Becka goaded. "You've just spent the past hour claiming that romance is truly dead."

"Yeah, well, it is." Frannie lifted her drink. "The trick to keeping romance alive is *not* to marry the guy when he asks. After the wedding gifts have been put away, it's *all* downhill." Her gaze rounded the table, resting on everyone's faces. "Am I right?"

"Honey, what you are," Diana murmured, "is over your limit."

Frannie looked as if she were going to take exception to that. But then she laughed. And nodded. "One drink's all it takes," she agreed. "I know. Call me bitter. It'll pass. Right, Faith? How long ago was your divorce?"

"Two years." Faith caught the waitress's attention, and signaled for a refill for their iced teas.

"Do you ever talk to Jess?" That came from Sharona.

"No." Faith handed over her glass when Juliet returned with the pitcher of tea. When she realized she was staring at the waitress's pregnant abdomen, she quickly averted her eyes. "Nothing to talk to him about. He remarried about two minutes after the ink was dry on our divorce papers." In the two years since, she figured her ex-husband's new wife had probably capably produced at least one child, if not more.

"When does it stop hurting?" Frannie stared at her over her fruity drink.

Faith murmured her thanks to Juliet after she'd finished filling the glasses, and the waitress flashed a pretty smile before moving off, her thick dark hair bouncing behind her shoulders. She thought about Frannie's question. "I don't know that I hurt about Jess anymore," she admitted. Jess had done what was best for him. And she hadn't been part of that package any longer.

It was the *reason* she wasn't suitable that hurt. She'd had a staph infection when she was a teenager. But not until she had failed to conceive with Jess and had grown concerned enough to seek a medical opinion had she learned the infection had left her so damaged.

"Puhleeze," Sharona drawled. "If you weren't still

hurting over that jerk's defection, then why on earth aren't you seeing other people by now?"

Faith eyed the other woman. "Maybe because I've been busy?"

"Not all of us have alimony settlements the size of yours," Becka added dryly, and the women laughed again. "Some of us actually have to work for a living."

"I'm dragging us all down," Frannie admitted. "Aren't I?"

"Yes," Diana agreed. But she winked. "We still love you anyway."

Frannie made a face. "Well, at least there's that."

Juliet returned with the check. "Anything else I can get you this afternoon?"

"You look like you should be sitting down here with *us* waiting on you." Tanya nodded her head at Juliet's expanding waistline. "I'll bet your feet are just killing you after your shift here."

Juliet's cheeks flushed a little, which seemed to make her liquid dark eyes sparkle even more. Her palm curved over the thrust of her abdomen. "Sometimes, a little," she admitted. "But everyone who comes in here is always so nice."

"Honey, I used to wait tables here—"

"—about a hundred years ago."

"—and I *know* not everyone who comes in here is nice," Becka continued, ignoring Sharona's interruption. She pointed at the painting hanging over the bar of a woman wearing nothing but strategically placed gauze. "And the Shady Lady there could attest to it."

Faith glanced up at the painting. She was so used

to seeing it there that she hardly noticed it anymore. But it did remind her that the bar and grill had once had a considerably more spicy reputation. "She probably shocked the hell out of the good townspeople in her day," she murmured. The painting wasn't lurid. But it was…suggestive.

Sharona reached out and took the check from Juliet. "Ladies. This lunch is on my third ex-husband." She produced a gleaming gold credit card. "God love him. My bank certainly does." She laughed.

Faith knew the laughter wasn't completely true, though. Every time Sharona married, she did it believing that it would last forever and a day.

Juliet took the credit card and check and disappeared again.

Becka lifted her iced tea. "Here's to another Valentine's Day sans a loving Valentine. Let's hope next year at least one or two of us is missing."

They all clinked glasses. Faith wondered if they were all wondering which of them would be there to share the day with old girlfriends.

She would probably be at the top of the list.

Which was just a little too much of a pity party to tolerate. She took a last drink of iced tea and stood. Hugged all of her friends, who were also gathering up purses and shopping bags and cell phones. Juliet returned, and Sharona was busy signing the charge slip.

Tanya hooked her arm through Faith's as they left the restaurant and headed to their cars. "So. *Are* you okay?" She clearly hadn't lost the thread of their whispered conversation.

"I didn't have nightmares about the search," Faith admitted as she reached her SUV and pulled open the door. She'd had dreams about Cameron *not* pulling back from her. And wasn't that the ultimate fantasy? "So, yeah. I guess I'm okay."

"Glad you came?"

Faith nodded. Tanya had goaded her into it, promising that if Faith didn't show at The Hitching Post, Sharona had threatened to come and haul Faith out of her condo by her toes. "I still have to make those cookies I promised Chris, though," she said. "I think he's planning to use 'em with the new residents. He told me yesterday that things are just going crazy at the hospital lately."

"I thought 'crazy' was standard operating procedure over there."

"Yeah. But he said it's been worse than usual." Faith shook her head a little. "You know, I've actually had two reporters come to me, wanting statements about the mine. *That* is what is crazy. I can't believe that gold fever is hitting this town. So, Toby's completely over his flu?"

Tanya nodded. "Thank goodness. I love that boy o' mine, but he isn't exactly the sweetest of patients."

"Give him a hug for me."

"Give Erik a hug for *me*." Tanya waited a beat, then laughed gently. "Oh, girl, you should see your face." She gave Faith a quick hug. "I'll talk to you later. I've gotta run into Bozeman. See if I can find some sexy lingerie that'll keep Derek awake for a few minutes tonight when he comes off duty." She wiggled her eyebrows and hurried toward her car.

Faith watched her go for a moment. Tanya was really lucky. She and Derek had fallen for each other the moment they'd laid eyes on one another when they were only seventeen years old. They'd married two weeks after graduating high school, throwing both sets of parents into fits. But here they were, fourteen years later—a child, a demanding career and a successful retail business later—still as giddy as newlyweds with one another.

Everyone should be so blessed.

She tilted back her head, looking up into the pristine blue sky. For the first time in weeks, she wasn't on call. She could have driven to Bozeman, too, if she'd wanted.

But she had a date with some flour and eggs and her oven.

And the fact that Erik and Cameron hadn't had much in the way of home-baked cookies didn't figure in at all to her unwarranted enthusiasm.

Four hours later, though, Faith's heart was in her throat and it irritated her to no end. So when she rapped her knuckles on the Stevensons' front door, the knock was a little louder than necessary.

She hoped Erik answered the door.

It would be *much* easier. She could hand over the frosted cookies to him, he'd probably be goggle-eyed over the prospect of a major sugar high, and she'd head on down the road again, giving her heart absolutely no reason to remain in her throat, threatening to make her pass out either from dizziness or from choking.

But the door wasn't yanked inward by the energetic boy.

It wasn't yanked inward at all.

She stood there staring at the firmly closed, heavy, dark wood-paneled door as her heart took a slow, anticlimactic slide back down where it belonged.

Well, what had she expected? It was Valentine's Day. Erik and Cam were probably out doing something…valentiney.

She smoothed her hand over the sealed box of cookies. She was *not* going to stand there and knock again. Not that there were any neighbors close enough to notice Faith loitering on the front porch. And even if there were, she figured her presence there on a Saturday afternoon was a lot less salacious than Cam calling for Todd to sit with Erik in the middle of the night.

She set the container on the slightly bedraggled welcome mat and went back down the steps to the snow-shoveled walk. She may have had plenty of fun at the grill that afternoon, and she may have enjoyed her baker stint, but now the evening stretched out in front of her with yawning emptiness.

She actually found herself wishing that her pager would go off, which was fine thinking, given that it took someone's safety being in jeopardy for her to be summoned.

And since she *wasn't* on call for once, why did she even have her pager on?

She fumbled with the car door, her bare fingers flinching from the cold metal. Maybe she'd take herself to a movie.

She abruptly nixed that idea. She ordinarily didn't mind going to a movie on her own. But on Valentine's Day? Major date night?

No thank you.

Two years ago, if she'd had time on her hands, she'd have kept them busy with crocheting. But she'd stopped crocheting when she'd started facing reality. Now, she just had a closet full of items that reminded her of what she couldn't have, that she used for baby shower gifts.

"Faith?"

Her fingers clenched around the edge of the door. She looked up. Cameron stood on his porch, the container of cookies in his hand. "I thought I heard the door," he said. "What's this?"

Her heart had taken its trip upstairs to her throat again.

She closed the car door and leaned against it. Maybe the chill penetrating her corduroy pants would keep some starch in her knees. "Cookies. You know. For Valentine's Day. I made too many. I could only pawn off so many on my brother. I thought maybe Erik would enjoy them." Which was a pretty blatant lie. Chris would happily have taken every single cookie. She just hadn't chosen to give them all to him.

Cam had flipped open the lid and was looking inside.

Her heart ached more than a little at the sight. Particularly when she knew good and well that she wouldn't be seeing him at all, if she hadn't taken this uncharacteristic step and approached him.

"He *will* love 'em," he said as he lifted out a bright pink-frosted heart and bit into it. "If there are any left by the time he gets home."

She realized she'd somehow traveled halfway up the walk again. "Gets home?"

"He's spending the night at Josh Lampson's."

Her jaw very nearly hit the concrete sidewalk. "He must be excited about that," she said cautiously.

Cameron shrugged, and something soft curled inside her because she knew the movement was not the casual thing he'd meant it to be. "I spoke with Josh's mom. She got switched the other day to a day shift. She'll be home all night tonight."

Faith took a few more steps. Cameron finished off the cookie in another bite, then licked his thumb, his glance sliding over her.

"Wanna come in?"

"Oh." She looked back at her car. "I, um—" Had nowhere else to go but home, she thought. And anywhere else to be that would be safer than being around him. "Sure. For a few minutes."

He cradled the container in his hand as if it were a football, and stood aside when she joined him on the porch, pushing the door inward. "After you."

She went inside, and silently chastised her foolish sense that entering his home felt different now than it had the other time she'd been there.

Just because Erik was gone—

She nearly jumped out of her skin when his fingers brushed her shoulders.

But he was only helping her out of her coat. She

quickly pulled her arms free and he hung it by the collar over the tree stand in the foyer that was already fat with several winter coats—some sized seven-year-old boy, and the rest sized full-grown man.

He passed her, his fingers poking inside the cookie container again. "Come on back. I was grading papers."

She realized he wore only socks on his feet. For some reason, it felt intimate seeing those scrupulously white, thick tube socks with a thin line of gold stitching over his toes.

"Seems you do a lot of that," she said very brightly, looking elsewhere. But "elsewhere" proved just as distracting. His hair had grown in the few weeks since the mine incident. Even in the few days since he'd come to her condo in the middle of the night because he'd *needed* to know she was okay.

And the rich, dark auburn strands did show a tendency to wave around his neck just as she'd suspected they would.

She surreptitiously rubbed her palms down the sides of her jeans. Cam slid the cookie container on the rectangular farmhouse-style table, and glanced back at her.

"Your hair's down."

She barely restrained lifting a self-conscious hand to her loose hair. "Guess it is. Is, um, that all stuff you have to grade?" She gestured toward the desk where papers were spread across the entire surface. A stack of folders, fat with assignments, she assumed, sat on one side. Two enormous textbooks were pushed to the other side. She also noticed a playbook among the mess.

"Yeah." His lips quirked a little. "And I used to complain about the massive amounts of paperwork back when I had my own finance firm." He picked up the slender bottle of beer he'd obviously been nursing, and tilted it. "Want one?"

She shook her head. His gaze was inscrutable, yet she still felt herself flushing at the steadiness of it on her face.

"That blue color's good on you," he said after a moment. "Got a date later?"

She *knew* she was blushing at that, which should have been ridiculous. "No."

"Why not? It's Valentine's Day. Evening," he corrected, as his gaze slid to the windows, which clearly showed the purposeful descent of the sun in a truly glorious display of fiery color.

"So?" She crossed her arms. Uncrossed them. "You're here doing schoolwork. Unless you're going out later," she added belatedly. He *had* let Erik spend the night at a friend's, after all. Which was highly unusual. Maybe he'd had a personal motivation behind that decision.

After all. He hadn't exactly answered her question about whether or not he'd been involved with anyone since his wife's death. Just because *she* couldn't think beyond him to another person, didn't mean he felt similarly toward her.

She was such a head case.

He plucked another pink cookie out of the container and demolished half of it in one bite, then followed it with a beer chaser and still his gaze stayed on her.

He'd looked at her that way the afternoon he'd kissed her, too. Before he'd backed away as if she were some sort of biohazardous material, that was. And he'd looked at her that way in her kitchen the other night. Before he'd put twelve feet of kitchen tiles between them.

"Do I have dirt on my face or something?" she finally asked, vaguely exasperated, as much from those particular memories as anything.

His lips quirked again, a little stronger this time. Enough to hint at the slash of a dimple he'd passed on to his son. He placed his bottle on the table, taking his time. "No. You don't have dirt on your face. No, I didn't ship off Erik for the night so I could go out later and score." His gaze burned over her face for a moment. "With anyone."

Her cheeks heated.

His lips tilted a little more. "You just look different."

"Great," she murmured. "That either means I'm barely presentable ordinarily, or I'm barely presentable now."

"Fishing for compliments?"

"No!"

He smiled outright, and the power of it bathed over her like seductive summer sunshine. "And do you know how to handle a compliment when it's given?"

"When I can tell it's a compliment," she countered.

So she'd changed into her brand-new blue turtleneck after her close encounter with her oven. So she'd dashed a little more makeup on than her usual smear of clear lip gloss. Next time, she wouldn't bother.

Next time?

What was she thinking?

"You look as beautiful as you always do." His deep voice had turned matter-of-fact. "Just different. So I figured you must have a reason. A date."

"I don't date." Which he undoubtedly had figured out for himself.

"Why is that?"

"Why do *you* care?"

"*You* asked me."

No. What she'd asked was whether he'd been with anyone in the years since Laura died. Definitely a different question. At least to her. But maybe not to him. And did it matter anyway?

Either way, the answer was *no*.

Silence ticked between them. She shook her head. "I should go." Before she made more of a fool of herself than she already had.

"What're you going to do?"

"I don't know." She wouldn't think about how she'd manage to fill the empty hours until she was on duty again. "Maybe make another batch of cookies so Erik might actually get one." She added some starch to her tone.

His lips tilted and he finished off the one still in his hand. "Wouldn't have taken you for a pastry chef."

She narrowed her eyes. "I told you I used to bake

with my mother and sisters. So, if that's an example of your compliments—"

He lifted his hand peaceably. "No. They're great. Which is clearly obvious. But to save you the extra work—" he deftly snapped the lid back on the container "—I'll preserve the rest for Erik. Good enough?"

"I like baking. It's nice to have a reason to do it." Her mind flitted to Erik's open house and she knew Cam was thinking about the same thing. Maybe his steady gaze wasn't quite as inscrutable as she'd thought. Which made all manner of warmth stir right back up inside her. "Well. I should let you get back to your work. Tell Erik I said happy Valentine's Day."

He nodded and she turned to go. She was halfway to the door when he spoke.

"I never did get a chance to give you that dinner. Why don't you stay and eat? I've got a couple of steaks ready to go."

She closed her eyes for a moment, blocking out the sight of his well-loaded coat tree that seemed to shout the fact it belonged to a family man. "I'm not sure that's a good idea," she admitted.

It wasn't his stockinged feet that alerted her to the fact that he was walking up behind her. It was the shiver that danced down her spine. The knot of breathless…waiting…that formed in her chest.

"Because Erik's not here?" His voice was as quiet as hers, and the low timbre dragged velvet-soft over her senses.

She exhaled carefully and turned to face him, only

to find him standing closer than she'd expected. Her nose practically grazed the thick, ivory knit of his bulky sweater. She slid back her foot, needing space. "Yes."

"If he were here, would you have stayed?"

She was trapped in his eyes, as surely as if he'd lassoed her. "I don't know," she admitted.

"He can wear a person out."

"He's energetic. And he undoubtedly got that from you, just like he got your hair and your eyes."

"Then why the hesitation?"

She wasn't even sure what they were talking about anymore. It was problematic, looking at a man who made one's ability for coherent thought fall right out the window.

"Not enough appeal unless my son is around?"

She shook her head. "You know that's not so." Her voice had gone husky again.

"Do I?"

Her entire body felt flushed. "I'm not the one who regrets kissing…touching…me." She pushed out the words.

His slashing eyebrows rose. "Regret. Believe me, darlin', I'm on intimate terms with regret, and that *isn't* what I've been feeling where you're concerned."

"Well, you could have fooled me." She hated that her voice wasn't steady. "Considering the way you—"

The rest of her words died under the swoop of his mouth catching hers.

Shock rocked through her, as deep and encompassing as it had the first time. Her fingers flexed. Grazed thick, cable knit. In shock's wake flowed need and pleasure. It spread through her, achingly warm, finding crevices that had been cold and empty.

His fingers tangled in her hair and her head fell back, her mouth opening under his. He made a low sound that rippled her nerve endings and her fingers curled around his forearms, kneading.

When he finally lifted his head, she sucked in a sharp breath, willing away the dizziness clouding her judgment. But she might just as well have tried jumping over the moon.

His hand surrounding the nape of her neck anchored her in place. "*This* is not regret," he rasped.

Faith trembled. "Cam—"

He kissed her again. Harder. More urgently. Only to break away again. His breathing was rough. "I want you. And you were right. It's been a long time. I haven't felt this way since my wife. And maybe I convinced myself that leaving you alone the other night was the right thing to do, but today I'm not feeling so generous. So if you really want to leave, do it now. Otherwise—" he grazed his thumb over her lips "—don't."

Chapter Eleven

Leave.

Don't leave.

A million thoughts whipped through Faith's head, but none of them stuck around long enough to gain form. "It would be smarter for me to go."

His thumb swirled over her chin. "Definitely."

"But I don't want to leave." The words were more exhale than form, but he seemed to understand all the same.

He stepped closer, his thumb raising her chin. His head dipped. But the racing urgency she'd expected didn't come. Instead, he brushed his lips over hers, a light exploration, a gentle discovering.

Her heart lurched. Her fingers twisted in his sweater.

When had she moved her hands to his chest?

She could feel the race of his heartbeat and it went to her head faster than the daiquiris had gone to Frannie's head that afternoon.

He kissed the corner of her mouth, the point of her chin, the line of her jaw.

She twisted her head, desperate for his mouth on hers. "Cam—"

His lips caught her earlobe and she shivered. His hand flattened over her spine, bringing her flush against him and a moan rose in her throat, her knees going soft.

He laughed silently, sounding so pleased with himself that she started to push at him, but he just covered her mouth again, tsking against her lips, and lifted her right off her feet, pulling her up his body until her mouth was even with his.

She clutched his shoulders and stared into his eyes. With no seeming effort at all, he held her there, his hands slowly sliding from her waist to her rear, her thighs.

Her legs circled his waist seemingly with a mind of their own and they both went still.

The only sound in the room was the rasp of her denim jeans against his, underscored by harsh breaths.

Then he swore under his breath, muttering an apology almost simultaneously, as he backed her against the knotty pine table right there in the foyer.

Envelopes and car keys flew under the haphazard swipe of his hand and he lifted his mouth only long enough to drag her sweater over her head. When it was gone, his palm covered her bare breast. His lips swallowed her gasping delight.

She pulled at his sweater, desperate to feel his skin against hers, and he obliged by tugging it off himself. Her blood hummed in her veins. Her mouth pressed against the satin warmth of his shoulder. Her breasts nestled against the crisp-soft swirl of hair on his chest. Her fingers blindly fumbled with the button at his waist, only to knock into his as he slid down *her* zipper.

"Hurry," she gasped.

And he swore, removing his hands from her altogether. And if she weren't pressed up against him so tightly, he'd have been inside her if not for a few layers of fabric.

She froze. "No. Not again. Don't pull away from me again."

His fingers circled her wrists, keeping her from touching him. "Dammit. I have to. What was I thinking?"

"Maybe I like you not thinking," she admitted unevenly. "Maybe I like you just...*being*. With me."

His jaw worked for a moment. "I want to. God. I want to. But I wasn't prepared... I—" he broke off, swearing. "No condom," he finally said, bluntly.

She stared. Felt the blood drain out of her face, only to return, double-speed. Hesitation niggled at her, but she stomped down hard on it. He might have her hands subdued, but he didn't have her legs.

She twined them more tightly around his hips and pulled him back. "We don't need one. Safe as houses, remember? Please, Cam. Do you want me to beg here?" She was so afraid she'd do just that. Hadn't she come bearing cookies in some barely disguised, antiquated gesture?

Her reserve was nil, and pride hadn't kept her from waking night after night from dreams of his hands touching her. So even though he'd pushed her away more than once, she'd still had to try.

His shackling grip had loosened just enough for her to slip one hand free, and she tugged at his jeans, popping the strained fly the rest of the way.

He groaned when she slid her hand over him. Touched him. Shaped him.

"Lift up," he rasped. She tilted her hips and he pulled the rest of her clothing free, dragging jeans and boots and socks off in one fierce motion. Then his hands, warm and so strong, slid up her thighs. "Are you sure, Faith?"

He'd called her Faith. She was shuddering wildly. "I'm sure." The words were little more than a moan, and she pressed her mouth against the hot column of his throat.

She felt—tasted—the groan he gave.

And then he sank into her.

Harder. Deeper. *More* than anything she'd ever experienced.

She cried out. Her head fell back, knocking the wall, but she barely noticed for the wild pleasure streaking through her.

His forehead fell to her shoulder, his hands like iron as he lifted her to him. "I don't want to hurt you."

She barely heard him. Her hands swept over his back, holding tight. "You're not," she promised. "Oh, Cameron."

His heartbeat felt like a locomotive pulsing against her breast. Her fingers flexed against him and she arched, mindlessly greedy, shocked in some small, tidy corner of her mind at the gasping moans coming out of her mouth, at the feral growl rising from him as he took.

And took.

And took.

He slapped a hand against the wall above her head. His mouth devoured hers, swallowing her cry. Everything inside her screamed for release.

The foyer table rocked precariously.

His mouth tore from hers. Burned to her temple. Her ear. His breath was harsh. "Faith."

Just that. Her name, so raw, so…perfect as she felt everything he was explode inside her.

And she shattered, too, flying apart.

She wasn't sure who was holding whom together more.

But in the end, it didn't really matter.

They were both destroyed, baptized in the fire of each other.

It wasn't really an eon of soul-deep pleasure, though it felt that way before Cam felt Faith go boneless against him, their bodies still fused. It was hardly a testament to his masculinity, but his damned legs were marshmallows. He blew out a shaking breath. Cautiously pushed his hand against the wall again, straightening away.

She clung like a limpet, her head tucked against his neck. "Don't go," she whispered hoarsely.

And damned if he didn't want her all over again, right then and there. "I'm not going anywhere." He sounded as if he'd run a marathon.

Maybe that's what happened when a man was outrunning his past.

He lifted her with him, managing to more or less collapse on the carpet without bruising either one of them.

He hoped.

She still had her head tucked against the crook of his neck, as if he'd been grown specifically for that purpose. Her long legs tangled with his.

And it all felt…right.

He tossed his arm over his eyes, slowly stroking her hair. "I still have on my pants," he muttered, feeling like a complete, lumbering jackass. It wasn't a sensation he was accustomed to, or one that he relished.

But *she* giggled. "I know."

Of all the sounds he'd elicited from her, it was the giggle that was the most unexpected.

And something inside him loosened. Unfurled. "I—"

"Wait." Her hand snuck up and covered his mouth. She lifted her head and looked at him. Her honey-colored hair drifted over them in silky sheaves. "If you apologize *now,* Cameron Stevenson, I'm very much afraid I might have to hurt you."

Her voice was humorous. But her eyes—more green than brown, and decidedly slumberous at the moment—were starkly vulnerable.

He stroked his knuckles over her smooth cheek.

Golden.

Touching her was like stepping into the warmest, most inviting, molten sunshine.

And he was so damn tired of being out in the cold.

Her lashes had flicked down, hiding her gaze when he'd touched her cheek.

"No. I can't apologize for that. Unless I left bruises or something." He moved his hand. Cupped her arms where he knew he'd grabbed her—probably too hard, too tight—and gently rubbed her satiny skin.

Her lashes lifted. "I don't bruise that easily," she whispered.

But he knew otherwise. Faith Taylor, competent, strong, beautiful Faith Taylor, just carried her bruises—whatever their cause—on the inside.

And he knew, the same way he'd known his life was forever changed the day he'd played checkers on a woolen blanket in a park, that he never wanted this woman bruised by anything. Ever.

He turned, settling her carefully on the carpet, and reached past her for his sweater. Then he held it out for her. She looked at him for a long moment before silently tucking her head through it.

For some reason, it seemed as trusting a gesture as what they'd done together in his foyer.

He pulled the sweater down around her. The ivory knit enfolded her past her hips. Then he rose. Fastened his jeans, fumbling a little at the avid way she watched him, and held out his hands. "Come on."

Her eyes narrowed a little. "Where?" But she settled her palms on his.

He pulled her to her feet. "So suspicious." And he'd given her plenty of reason to be. "I want to show you something."

"What? Your etchings? Think maybe we've covered that already."

He gave a bark of laughter at that. "You'll see."

He drew her back down the hall to the great room. Past his desk, past the windows that looked over the hill where she'd tobogganed with Erik, and into the den beyond. "I was in here when you knocked," he told her. "That's why I didn't hear you."

Her gaze was traveling over the burgundy leather couches and the massive bookcase built into the wall that was already overflowing with books. The fire he'd built earlier that day was nothing but a smolder now, and he tossed another log on, jabbing it with the poker, making sparks fly up the chimney. A fresh scent of wood smoke curled into the room.

He replaced the black iron screen and turned to Faith. "I was watching that." He gestured at the big-screen television mounted on the wall, but she'd already noticed the frozen image of Erik from the night of the school's chorus program. He picked up the remote and pushed Rewind. "You were there only long enough to see the last ten minutes or so."

Her fingertips were curled around the edges of his sweater sleeves. She cast him a sideways look. "How'd you know when I came in? I was in the back."

He handed her the remote and slid a long lock of her hair free of the sweater collar. "I noticed. Same way I always noticed when you'd come in the council meetings. When you snuck out a few minutes before it ended. When you climbed up in the bleachers at the last game. I noticed."

Her lips parted softly. Her thumb roved restlessly over the buttons on the remote, not pushing any of them. "Oh."

His lips twitched. "Yeah. *Oh.*" He gestured at the furniture. "Make yourself comfortable. I'm just gonna heat up the grill."

She looked thoroughly bemused and he wondered how long he'd be able to keep her in that state. She sat down on the corner of the couch, curling her long legs beneath the hem of his sweater, and pointed the remote to start the video playing again.

He went into the mudroom and grabbed a shirt off the pile of laundry he'd yet to put away, and pushed his feet into his boots, then went out on the deck to flip on the grill. He left it to heat and went back inside. Steaks were a no-brainer, fortunately. And these days the salad came conveniently out of a bag.

Thank God for modern conveniences.

He dumped it into a bowl, scooping what he spilled on the counter into the trash. Then he hastily scrubbed a few potatoes, stabbed 'em a couple of times and tossed them in the microwave, punching the button that said…ta daa…*potato*. Another major convenience, since the only way he'd learned his way around the kitchen was by trial and error. He pulled out the steaks, went back to the deck and slapped them on the grill, then closed the domed lid over them and went back inside.

"Gourmet touches." Faith stood in his kitchen looking more edible than anything he could have imagined. She held up the emptied bag from the salad between two fingers. "I've never had a man cook for me before."

"Oh yeah?" He dropped the long-handled fork he'd used with the steaks onto the counter and headed for her. "Stand around looking like that, Faith, and I'll be happy to cook *any*time."

Her eyes widened and her lips curved. "Cam—"

"Keep saying my name," he suggested gruffly as he slid an arm around her waist, delving oh-so-easily beneath the sweater. He pushed his other hand through her silky hair and her head fell willingly to the side, letting him taste the skin right below her ear.

"Cam." That came a little more breathlessly.

He caught her earlobe gently between his teeth.

"Cah…ham." Her hands grazed his chest. "The, um, the video is rewound."

He heard her. He just didn't hear her. "I'm not ever going to get enough of you." He widened his stance, pulled her closer. Tighter.

She wriggled against him, pushing at his shoulders. "The, um, the *video?*"

He exhaled. Pressed his forehead to hers. "Right." He took in another long breath. Let it out even more slowly. Reluctantly let go of her. "Bright idea of mine," he muttered. "You deserve candlelight and champagne. I serve up nuked potatoes and home movies."

Her eyes softened even more. "I've never had much of a head for champagne, actually. And I don't…expect romantic gestures."

He looked at her. "You said something like that before," he remembered. When he'd conveniently used her to derail the threesome at The Hitching Post. "Don't you believe in romance?"

"Of course I do." She dropped the empty sack on the counter. "I just don't think I'm the kind of woman who brings that out in anyone."

He nearly laughed out loud until he realized she was serious. "You must have been married to a prize idiot," he murmured, slipping his hands along her neck. Watching the way her lips parted unconsciously as he pressed his thumb against the pulse fluttering at the base.

"I suppose you treated your wife to grand gestures all the time."

"No," he said, and for once the honesty didn't scrape raw and painful at his insides. "She was the one who was into gestures. I was the practical one who cleaned up the mess afterward."

"Mess. Ah. Well. There you go. Grand gestures *must* be overrated if they leave a mess."

He closed in on her, following her as she backed up, until she was caught between him and the undoubtedly cool front of his stainless steel fridge. "Yeah, darlin', but I've learned that some things are worth a mess." He leaned down and nipped at her lower lip, watching her face.

Her eyes glazed, turning more green than brown again in the moment before they started to close.

"Come on," he whispered. "Let's go watch the video."

Faith pressed her lips together, scrambling for composure. "You enjoy keeping me off balance, don't you?"

He nibbled her lip again. "Gotta take my advantages where I can…against the superior species."

She started to smile, remembering the snowball fight when she'd jokingly assured him females *were* superior. But the fact of the matter was Cam needed no special effort to throw her off balance. All he had to do was *be*.

Thank heavens his heart was still tied to his wife.

If it weren't, Faith could never let herself be with him this way. It would just be too dangerous. Too painful when he ended it. And end it he would, if he knew about her infertility.

She lifted her mouth more fully to his, pushing the thoughts away. Hard. "How long are those steaks going to take?"

"Not long enough," he murmured.

Still, he kissed her slowly.

Thoroughly.

Until she was in danger of melting right into the floor beneath her bare feet. Then he walked her back to his den. Settled her on that sinfully soft leather couch.

Picked up the remote.

Hit Play.

And sat in the chair opposite her. His eyes were sharp. Amused. Aroused.

She exhaled. Focused on the mammoth television set.

In minutes, she was entranced all over again by the children and managed to forget—mostly—the fact that Cam watched her far more than he watched the video.

When it came time for Erik's solo, she hit Rewind twice. Fortunately, Cam had gone to the kitchen again to attend to dinner, after giving her strict instructions to stay put.

She did, with one quick foray to find a bathroom.

In her exploration, though, she found Cam's bedroom.

The bed was mammoth. No real surprise there. Cam would need a good-size bed. He was a good-size man, after all. It was covered with a thick, caramel-colored comforter with a few brown pillows tossed haphazardly on top. And it was made.

Which was more than she could say for her own considerably smaller, full-size bed at home, which she'd left in kicked-about disarray from her restless nights of late.

It was the photographs on the dresser as she crossed to the attached bathroom that grabbed her attention, though.

They gave Faith her first look at Laura Stevenson. And Cam's wife had been stunning.

There was just no other word for her. Clouds of black hair. Violet eyes so vivid they seemed to leap from the photographs. She'd had curves where Faith had never had them, and the adoration between her and the man beside her was tangible.

But as curious—and yes, daunted—as she'd been about Laura, it was Cam's image that really stopped

Faith in her tracks, making her actually pick up the sterling-framed photograph to look closer.

His hair had been brutally short, but the severe style simply played up his carved features. Maybe made him look a little older than he would actually have been at the time the photograph was probably taken. And the suit he wore looked as if it belonged on the cover of *GQ*.

It was Cameron. Yet…it wasn't the Cam she knew.

The Cam who padded around his house in tube socks and jeans and—her hand drifted down the front of his thick sweater that was all she still wore—who'd pelted his son with snowballs.

She settled the photograph carefully back in place, well aware that she was intruding in his personal space, no matter *what* they'd done together in his foyer, and quickly used his bathroom. She was hurrying back to the den when he appeared in the hallway opposite her, a large wooden tray held in his hands.

She froze, feeling ridiculously guilty. "I, um, used your bathroom. Hope you don't mind."

His eyebrows drew together a little bit, almost as if he were curious why she'd even have to ask. "Better mine than Erik's," he said after a moment. "Kid's a slob no matter what I tell him." He gestured a little with the laden tray. "Come on. We'll eat by the fire."

She went into the den. He set the tray on the iron coffee table in front of the couch and then sat down beside her. He grabbed the remote and punched a few buttons. The video turned off. The television slid down, disappearing into the rustic pine cabinet beneath it.

She slid a glance his way. "You definitely don't live like any other teachers I know."

He smiled a little. "Nice to know the law, business and accounting degrees went to *some* good."

She tugged at her ear a little. "So, um, what are your parents like?"

He handed her a plate buried under by steak, salad and potato. "Conservative. Old money." His lips quirked. "As old as Denver goes, at any rate. They had me when they were both over forty. No brothers or sisters, either. By mutual agreement, we see as little of each other as humanly possible, and mostly only for holidays. Dad didn't take too kindly to it when I didn't join his brokerage, but put out my own shingle. I actually became his competition." He sliced off a corner of steak and studied the pink center for a moment. "They raised me to have my own brain, and didn't want me to use it." He shook his head a little, then ate the meat. "Last time I heard from him, it was to tell me he'd gotten Erik accepted into my old private school."

Alarm halted her fork as she stabbed it into the fluffy potato. "You're not going to send him to boarding school, are you?"

He shook his head. "No. That was never the plan."

Relieved, she poked at the potato a little more, letting some of the heat escape. "And that plan is to raise him in Thunder Canyon," she confirmed quietly. "Laura's plan."

His gaze was suddenly inscrutable. "Yeah."

"Do you like living here, Cam?" She couldn't bear to think that maybe he did not.

"Do you?"

She nodded immediately. "There was a time when I was perfectly anxious to leave it, of course." She grinned wryly. "I was eighteen and ready to grab the world by the tail and swing it around my head a few times."

"And now?"

She tasted a corner of steak, and stared into the fire across from them for a moment as she savored the bite. A little crispy on the outside. A lot juicy on the inside.

"Now," she said eventually, "I can't really imagine living anywhere else." Thunder Canyon had welcomed her home when her world had been in tatters. It had healed her.

Had it?

She ignored the unwelcome query and caught Cameron watching her when she looked at him. "And you still haven't answered the question," she pointed out.

"I don't know."

She lifted her eyebrows. "You must have some opinion. You're not exactly without one when it comes to most matters. I've heard you at those council meetings, remember?"

He smiled wryly at the jab. "I haven't thought a lot about what I feel about Thunder Canyon," he said after a moment. "I've been…going through the motions."

"Doing what you believed Laura would have wanted you to do," she finished quietly.

"Yeah."

His gaze shifted to the fire and Faith wondered if he was envisioning his beautiful, black-haired wife.

She set down her fork, her ravenous appetite suddenly gone. "You know, maybe it's none of my business, but it seems to me that for a guy who's living his life to someone else's desires, you're doing an awfully good job of it."

"What?"

"Well." She turned sideways on the couch, tugging the sweater over her knees. "Just that you could have stayed here in Thunder Canyon, raising Erik here and all, without going to the measures that you have. I mean, you don't *have* to be the coach at school. You clearly didn't even *have* to become a teacher, for that matter. And the mayor wants you to run for town council. You actually told him you'd consider it. Pretty involving stuff, that's all." And she wasn't at all sure how he'd react to her opinion.

He turned a little on the couch, too, his arm stretching across the back of it. He lifted a lock of her hair and slowly flipped it through his fingers. And all he said in response to her observation was a low "hmm."

But the glint in his eyes was unmistakable and heat slid through her with the subtlety of a bulldozer. "I, um, I should probably be going."

He shook his head once. "It's cold out."

"It's February," she said dryly.

His lips twitched. "And you brought Valentine's Day dessert."

She shot a look at his plate. He'd eaten more than she had, but his plate was still half full. "I'm sure you'd tell Erik that he had to eat more of his supper before you'd let *him* have a cookie."

His smile widened. He leaned forward, grasping her arms and easily pulling her right over to him. She caught her breath as he swept his hands beneath the sweater.

"Who mentioned cookies? I was talking about you."

He kissed her, and didn't stop until they were both breathless.

Then he pushed to his feet, lifting her right along with him, and carried her down the hall to his bedroom. When he reached the bed, he leaned over, swept back the comforter, sending the pillows bouncing to parts unknown, and settled her in the center.

The room was dimmer now. The sun had set. The only illumination came from the hallway. But there was enough that she could see the look on his face as he slowly pulled off his clothes.

Faith tucked her tongue between her teeth, unable to look away from him. He was so incredibly beautiful.

"Something wrong?" His voice was amused.

"Not a thing," she assured faintly.

He smiled a little, then knelt next to the bed. He curled his warm hands around her ankles and slowly pulled her back across the bed toward him. She moved. The sweater, however, stayed put, until it rode up above her waist. Her breasts.

"I'll never unwrap another present and not think of you," he murmured, watching the progress of the sweater.

She swallowed, steeped in the warmth of his gaze as he pressed his lips to the curve of her knee.

His palms slid over her thighs. Reached up to her hips. The nearly healed scrapes. "Do they still hurt?"

She slowly shook her head. "Not anymore."

His right eyebrow peaked. "Supposed to say that they do," he murmured, sin and temptation wrapped up in that low, husky tone. "So I'd have to kiss 'em better."

She exhaled. "Oh." Then swallowed as he moved. "I…ah…think you're doing that anyway."

He lifted his head for a moment, his brown gaze colliding with hers. "Observant, aren't you?"

Her legs shifted, restless as his lips roved over the point of her hipbone. She pulled at his shoulders, but the man was immovable. "Cameron."

He leisurely pressed his mouth against her navel. "Mmm?"

He was maddening. Playing her as skillfully as if he'd written a playbook designed just for her. "Cam."

"Yeah." His lips moved against her. His palms pushed on her thighs as he slid forward.

Her head fell back against the mattress as he found her. Took her. Just that smoothly.

Just that easily.

Just that perfectly.

Her arms circled him, and she opened her mouth against his. His name sighed through her mind.

And then she thought no more.

Chapter Twelve

Faith wasn't aware of falling asleep. Not until she woke when the cool dawn light curled into the room and the warm weight of Cam shifted beside her.

She turned on her back. His elbow was bent on the mattress beside her head, his chin propped on his hand and she reached up, smoothing back the hair that was falling over his forehead. "Hi," she whispered.

"I was watching you sleep."

She let her hand trail down his face, his jaw. Rub against the hair on his chest for the sheer pleasure of feeling it against her palm. "Hope I wasn't drooling."

He chuckled softly. Leaned down and kissed the tip of his nose. "That would've been me, looking at you."

She smiled faintly.

Then he touched her hand and warmth crept up her arm, soothing. Seductive. She couldn't have moved if her life depended on it. Nor did she want to move. Her palm slowly flattened, barely grazing against his.

The warmth reached her shoulders. Drifted through her bloodstream, thawing. Steeping. "Cameron—"

"Shh." His thumb slid along hers. Traced up her index finger. Pressed gently against her fingertip, then slid down, and up her middle finger.

Her heart thudded heavily. She turned toward him, her leg sliding over his. "We probably shouldn't have done this," she whispered.

"Regrets already?" His fingers slowly slid through hers, bringing their palms flush against each other, snug and warm, steady and strong.

Did she regret being with him? She slowly shook her head. "No."

His fingers slowly released hers, only to run down the inside of her wrist. She swallowed. His fingers dipped to the inside of her elbow, then retraced the burning path back to her wrist. Her pulse thudded erratically against his fingers when he paused over it.

"Your skin is so soft." His low, deep voice rolled over her, as sensitizing as his fingertips. "Here." He dragged the palm of his hand back down her arm, then up to her shoulder.

Her breathing stalled.

"And here." He smoothed over her collarbone. Cupped the base of her neck. "Here." Her breasts tightened when he flattened his hand against her chest, thumb and little finger grazing the inner swell of them as he followed a straight line down to her navel.

Her abdominal muscles jumped. He sucked in an audible breath and his fingers slid again. Tightened against her waist, turning her toward him more fully.

A soft sound escaped her lips. She pressed her forehead against the hot curve between his shoulder and neck. Her hands drifted over the supple skin stretching over his ribs. His hand cupped the base of her neck, tilting her head back until his mouth found hers, lingered, then moved on to her temple. Her ear.

She sighed, lost in pleasure.

"I could get used to this."

His voice was a low murmur through the haze clouding her senses. "Mmm-hmm."

He tipped her onto her back again, and threaded his hands through her hair, spreading it out around her shoulders. She finally opened her eyes only to find him looking at her. "What? I'm drooling now?"

He shook his head. "I could get used to this," he repeated. "Not just you in my bed. But you. In my life."

Her breath stuttered. Stopped. She flattened her palms against the mattress, and pushed herself up against the rough-hewn headboard. "Cam—"

"No. Let me get this out." He caught her hands in his. Even in the dim light, she could see the muscle that had begun to tick in his jaw. "I never thought I'd be able to say that to another woman, Faith. But you—"

"You don't have to say anything, Cameron." Her voice was quick. Nervous. And there seemed nothing she could do to modulate it. "I haven't...had sex since my divorce. You haven't had sex since Laura died."

His eyes narrowed. "I've had plenty of *sex* since she died," he said flatly.

"But you said you hadn't felt this way since your wife."

"Felt," he said evenly. "Not just working off some sexual steam. But that's what you thought this was, didn't you? Scratching some damn itch? Fulfilling some damn need?"

She flinched at the hard note in his voice. She couldn't back up any more than she had, since her spine was already plastered against his headboard. "No." She struggled with words, knowing none of them would be right. "You know you're special to me, Cam." A monstrous understatement, but all she was capable of uttering when panic was turning her inside out. "You have to know that by now. This isn't...typical of me."

His gaze didn't waver from her face. His tone gentled. "Well...maybe we need to make this more typical. You. Me. Together."

His hands curled more tightly around hers, as if he'd read the frantic, futile messages screaming inside her head for her to pull her hands free. She stared at him, mute.

"Faith, until you, I never thought I'd even be able to contemplate a future that included another woman. That I'd ever consider marriage again. More children."

Her breath suddenly whistled between her teeth. She was actually getting dizzy. She concentrated hard on his face, but it was the only thing in her vision that didn't seem blurry. "No. No. This isn't... You're just—" she wheezed "—overreacting."

"Holy Chri—" He bit off the curse. "You're hyperventilating." He was off the bed in a flash.

She leaned over, gasping, struggling for breath.

This could not be happening.

He returned almost immediately, a small paper lunch sack in his hand, and stuck it over her mouth. "Breathe." His hand smoothed over her spine.

Tears burned out the corners of her eyes. She cupped the bag to her mouth. Breathed into it.

"There you go. Slow and easy." His hand swept down her bowed spine.

Her dizziness slowly faded, only to leave exhaustion in its wake.

"That's it. Just relax." He kept stroking her back. Again. And again.

And the fact that she wanted to stay there, wanted to have him touching her, in passion, in tenderness, in…anything and everything, made her slowly lift her head.

To sit up.

To face him.

His hand slowly fell away.

There were faint red marks on his shoulders. Not scratches. But definitely marks from her own fingers. His bed—the bed he'd undoubtedly shared with the beloved wife he'd lost—was more than tumbled. The bottom sheet was hanging on to the mattress by little more than a prayer.

Panic had ripped through her.

Exhaustion now dragged at her.

And, as she looked at Cameron, her gaze taking in the rest of the room beyond him—complete with the collection of family photographs on his dresser—she could feel a great wave of grief building on the horizon.

He's a family man.

You knew it, and you didn't stay away.

She shook her head, even as her hand crept up and grazed the soft bristles blurring his hard jaw. "I can't do this, Cam."

His jaw flexed against her palm and she went to draw away, but he grabbed her hand, holding it there. Tight. "Why?" His voice was raw. As raw as she felt inside.

Oh, what a fool she was. She was supposed to help keep people safe. And now she was only causing pain. To her. To him.

But it was better to do it now, rather than later.

Wasn't it?

"I'm not cut out for…you know. Relationships."

He snorted and swore. "That's bull."

She felt the blood drain out of her head again, and worked her hand free of his. "I don't have to convince you."

If she could only convince herself.

She slid off the mattress, away from him, and blindly swept around for her clothes only to realize they were still lying near the front door. She bunched the sheet around her body, and headed for the doorway.

"Don't."

She tripped a little. Snatched up the offending edge and moved faster.

"Faith."

She couldn't look back to see if Cam followed her.

If she looked back, she'd weaken. And if she weakened, she'd agree to anything he suggested. Anything, as long as she had him in her life.

One step at a time.

She just had to get through one step at a time.

Yank on her jeans.

Pull her sweater over her head.

She made the mistake of glancing up.

Cam stood there. His eyes narrowed. His arms crossed over his wide chest. He'd pulled on his jeans, too, but they were only half-fastened.

She left the sheet on the floor where it lay. Grabbed up her purse. Fumbled with her boots, only to give up and just clasp them to her chest.

She scrambled with the door, and tore out into the frozen dawn as if the devil was at her heels.

But it was just a man who was behind her. A good, decent, family man, who had the tools in his very being to break her heart.

And if she stayed—oh, God, if she stayed—when that day came, she wouldn't survive it.

Not this time.

The sidewalk burned so cold against her feet as she ran to her SUV. When she climbed behind the wheel, she dropped the keys twice in her fumbling attempt to get them in the ignition.

Then the engine caught. Roared like some beast in pain.

She looked back at the house.

He stood on the porch.

She hauled in a breath, only it sounded more like a sob.

And the sight of him wavered because of the tears flooding her eyes.

She shoved the SUV into drive and flattened her foot on the gas pedal. The vehicle shot forward.

Some portion of her mind was coherent enough to be grateful for the empty streets courtesy of the early hour on a Sunday morning. Because she managed to make it to her condo without mishap.

The phone was ringing even before she made it inside. Had obviously been ringing a number of times. And the message light was already blinking.

The ringing stopped. Cam's voice came on. "I don't know what's going on, Faith, but you better damn well tell me you made it home safely, or I'm coming over even though you've made it *more* than plain that you don't want to see me." His voice was tight. Angry.

Hurt.

She picked up the phone. "I'm home."

"Good."

He hung up.

She cupped the phone against her stomach and slowly slid down the wall until she was sitting on the floor. Eventually, the phone started beeping.

She pressed the button, disconnecting the call.

Then she lay down on her side.

And cried.

Cameron stared at the phone sitting on his desk.

His hand reached out to pick it up again. To call her again. To tell her anything that would get her back.

Might as well try to rewind the past twenty-four hours. He'd have as good a chance of success.

He shoved himself out of his chair and it rolled back, tipping on two wheels and crashing over, knocking hard into the wall. A framed oil painting Laura had picked up at an estate sale the first year they were married slid straight down, bouncing off the base of the chair and landing flat on the floor.

He exhaled roughly. Started to just leave it there. He'd never liked the painting, with its fussy strokes and jarring colors. But Laura had loved it.

And he'd loved her.

Loved.

He raked his hands through his hair and slowly went over to the painting. Crouched down and set it upright against the wall.

He'd *loved* Laura.

He'd made a life here in Thunder Canyon that would have made her happy.

But that was all in the past.

She'd died. And he was finally starting to feel alive again.

He pinched the bridge of his nose, digging his fingers into the pain that squatted malevolently behind his eyes.

And the woman responsible for shoving him into the land of the living couldn't face the mere idea of a relationship with him without coming unglued.

He straightened and left the painting leaning against the wall.

Living again sucked.

Chris Taylor stared at his sister's blond head and struggled hard to keep the worry out of his voice as he leaned his hip against the corner of her desk at the fire station. "You going to drive in to Bozeman for the basketball game tonight?"

She didn't look up from the report she was typing. "I'm on call," she finally answered. "And half the town is heading over there, anyway." She finally cast him a look. "Is that the pressing question that dragged you over here?"

"We were supposed to have lunch today remember?"

Her expression told him clearly enough that she hadn't. "Sorry," she mumbled, and looked back at her computer screen.

He sighed mightily. He'd waited for her at The Hitching Post for twenty minutes before realizing she wasn't going to show. Only thing he'd accomplished while he was there was getting Juliet Rivera off her feet for about ten minutes. As far as he was concerned, the young woman needed to be off her feet permanently until her baby made its appearance.

He straightened off Faith's desk and grabbed the side chair nearby to pull it up closer. He sat down.

Grabbed the arms of her chair and physically turned her until she was facing him. "Talk."

"There's nothing to talk about."

"Yeah. Right." He kept her from turning her chair back toward her desk. "Not so easy. I want to know what's going on. Mom called me last night. Said you sounded weird on the phone the other day when she tried calling you. Jill called me this morning to complain about you forgetting to mail her one of those crocheted baby blankets of yours for her girlfriend's shower, and she said you hung up on her when she bitched at you about it. So what gives?"

"Nothing is going on." She reached forward and pinched the inside of his arm, hard. He yelped and let go of her seat. She turned back to her desk. "Absolutely nothing, and that is exactly the way I want it."

"This is about the coach."

She typed, but he could see on the screen that it was more gobbledygook than words. "This is about *nothing*."

"Yeah, that washes real well, kiddo."

She glared at him.

Chris saw the glisten in his sister's eyes, though, and stifled a sigh. "They're just worried about you," he said quietly. *They,* hell. *He* was worried, too. But telling Faith that wouldn't do him any good. "Saw Erik Stevenson today," he said deliberately.

At that, her eyes widened, her attention definitely on him. "Is he okay?"

"Yeah. Just a follow-up visit."

Her relief was palpable.

"He was full of talk about how his dad signed him up for rock climbing over at Tanya's place," he added.

Her eyebrows shot up. "He did?"

"Haven't talked to Tanya much this week, either, have you?"

Her eyebrows lowered. "It's been a busy week."

And his sister was hiding out from the world. "He's also signed the kid up for Little League baseball," he informed her. "You know, Faith, I'm sorry about what Jess put you through. But he was a selfish jerk. He was selfish before you married him. And he was selfish after you were unmarried. You can't have kids. I know. I'm sorry. But there are a lot of people a helluva lot worse off than you."

Her brows drew together, stricken. "I know that."

"Do you?" He dragged her chair around again. "Word around town is that you and the coach haven't been seen in the same five-block radius since last week."

Her lashes swept down, but not quickly enough to hide the stark pain in them, and his irritation dissolved. "Do you love him?"

"*What? No!* Of course not."

Methinks she doth protest too much, he thought. "Okay. Just asking."

She slid her attention back to her computer. "Stop asking. There's nothing to say."

He rubbed his thumb down her arm. "You still haven't told anyone, have you. About the infertility."

Her face turned red. She eyed him. "No, but if you don't keep your voice down, anyone passing through the station here will know."

"It's nothing to be ashamed of. You had a staph infection, Faith. When you were a teenager. Nobody could have predicted the effect it left behind."

"Nobody could have predicted," she agreed tightly. "And I'm not infertile. I'm sterile. A revelation that made Jess immediately start looking for a new wife who *could* produce kids. End of story. And Cam…"

He waited.

She exhaled through her teeth. "Sooner or later— probably sooner, given the things he said—he's going to want more children. And I can't give that to him. And I can't watch another man I lo—*care* about, walk away from me because of *my* failure."

He wanted to latch on to the word she wouldn't let herself say just as much as he wanted to throttle her for the word she *had* said. Failure. "You're physically incapable of producing a child," he said—quietly, because he wouldn't entirely put it past Faith to pound him if he didn't. "It's a fact, not a failure." And it was a fact *he* knew, only because at her most desperate, she'd sought his professional opinion.

"Well, I've dealt with it as much as I intend to."

He stood. "Honey, you haven't dealt with it, at all. If you had, you wouldn't still be keeping it a secret." He glanced around the station house where a half-dozen firefighters were moving around doing various tasks from filing to polishing the inside of the windows. "And I don't mean from these guys. I mean from Mom and Dad. From our sisters. From the man you lo—" He hesitated deliberately, watching her eyes widen as if daring him to say it. The pager at his waist buzzed, and he automatically pulled it free to check the display.

Lunchtime was over.

"How're the new residents coming along?"

He took pity, allowing her dogged change of subject. "I'm surviving them. One's got an attitude that Thunder Canyon isn't exactly the pinnacle of medical achievements."

"Too bad you can't tell him to take a hike."

"Her." A damned pretty her, at that.

He leaned down and kissed the top of Faith's head, putting Dr. Zoe Hart *out* of his head. "Don't let Jess's failure where you two were concerned control your future, Faith. Maybe you might think about that."

He left, sketching a wave at the fire truck that was just pulling in from a call.

His pager buzzed again.

He sighed a little and quickened his step.

The E.R. seemed to be getting busier with each passing day, and every other person who came through seemed to be running a temperature fueled by gold fever.

The distinctive yellow school buses passed Faith on the highway between Bozeman and Thunder Canyon shortly after midnight.

Standing well off the side of the road next to her SUV with Jim Shepherd, she stared after the taillights until they dwindled to nothing in the dark.

"Probably your basketball team," Jim murmured, handing a coil of nylon rope over to her.

She nodded and tucked it away in the back of her SUV. She didn't want to wonder how the team had done.

She wondered anyway.

So she focused harder on the task at hand. They'd already loaded up Jim's equipment. Their engines were running, sending wisps of white exhaust curling into the night. "Maybe it'll help cut down on lost cross-country skiers when Caleb Douglas gets that ski resort of his up and running. At this point, I think we're close to breaking a record on this kind of call."

"Might be." Jim tugged at his ear for a moment. "You doing okay?"

The slick fabric of the SAR jacket she'd bought to replace the one she'd had to leave in the Queen of Hearts rustled as she closed her tailgate. "Why wouldn't I be?"

Her boss shrugged. "You just seemed preoccupied."

"I'm sorry. Won't happen again."

He let out a breath. "Faith, it wasn't a judgment on your performance. In another year, you'll probably be the ranking member. I was just asking."

She hesitated. "I'm fine. Really. I just…have a few personal issues to deal with."

"Well. If you want to talk, you know where I am."

She nodded. Watched him walk toward his truck and climb in. But he waited until she'd gotten into her own vehicle and turned it toward Thunder Canyon before he set off in the opposite direction.

Her hands tightened around the steering wheel. Talk. Maybe it made her the biggest coward on the planet, but she just didn't want to talk. What was the point of talking about something that could not be changed?

Her foot pressed harder on the accelerator, and intentionally or not, she soon had the three buses within eyesight, again.

She hung back, though, just following along. She had the scanner turned down low, but not so low that she didn't hear Cheryl's chatter about the game.

Cam's team had won.

Faith's hands tightened around the wheel a little more. She had no difficulty imagining the celebration that would occur upon their return. It was a wonder the buses weren't simply floating home.

The highway headed uphill and the buses slowed some, laboring against the grade while her SUV ate it up. She flicked her blinker and passed the first bus. Through the windows, she could see arms waving, hats flying.

The same was true of the second bus, and the one in the lead, when she passed that one, too.

She even saw Erik, who noticed her. He pulled down the window as far as it would go and stuck his head right out, waving madly, his hair whipping around his head like mad.

Aching inside, she waved, too.

Then a long arm scooped Erik's head back inside the window. Faith caught a glimpse of Cam's face. He eyed her for a moment.

Then slid the window up.

Headlights were in the oncoming lane and Faith accelerated, passing the bus and moving back into her own lane.

But she was shaking.

Cam hadn't even smiled.

What did you expect?

She drove the rest of the way back to town, feeling as if Cam's dark eyes were boring into the back of her spine. It wasn't on her way, but she found herself passing The Hitching Post, all the same. The place was still lit up. Cars lined the street and filled the lot.

She fully intended to drive on by. To go home. To fold herself in a blanket in the corner of her couch and pretend that she would be able to sleep, the same way she'd done for the past five nights.

She drove around the lot. Made herself a parking spot where there was none.

Inside, the grill was already packed. Many had clearly already returned from the game. If there was a patron in the grill who *wasn't* a basketball fan, she figured they would quickly become one, or they'd quickly be escorted to the door.

"Hey." Tanya grabbed her elbow. "Didn't expect to see you. Toby and I are over in the corner, but we can make some room for you. Did you find the skier?"

Faith shrugged out of her slick coat and followed her friend. "Yeah. Safe and sound, but cold. We sent him to the hospital for a look-see." She pointed at an empty bar stool near a group of people. They waved at it, and she carried it over to Tanya's small round table. If she craned her neck a little, she could see the door. She'd see when the team came in and escape through the back.

"Oh, man." Toby's sparkling brown eyes were fastened on someone across the room. "Look at Polly Caruthers. She is so suh-wheet." He slid off his stool, all long legs and gangling arms. "Gotta go, Ma."

Tanya rolled her eyes. "I'm Ma, now. Lovely, huh?" But she was smiling. "Kids. Gotta love 'em. Even when they're twelve-year-old boys who've discovered girls don't have cooties after all."

Faith toyed with one of the round cardboard coasters sitting in the center of the table. "Speaking of kids," she said slowly.

A tall waitress rushed by the table, settling a glass of water in front of Faith. "What can I get you?"

A vat of courage?

She ordered a diet cola. Figured it would be easier to obtain.

"Speaking of kids," Tanya prompted after the woman scurried off, menus tucked under her arm and an empty tray in her hand. "What about them?"

Faith flipped the coaster over. Took a deep breath. Expelled it in a rush. "I can't have any," she said bluntly.

Tanya blinked. "Excuse me?"

"Don't make me repeat it," Faith said thickly.

"Oh, honey." Tanya covered her hand with hers. "Just because you and Jess didn't…" Her voice trailed off at the look Faith gave her. Realization hit. "Oh. *Oh.*" She grimaced. "Well, that schmuck. He never was good enough for you."

The last thing Faith expected to do was to laugh. But she did. It came out a little rusty, but it still came. "Sure. You say that now."

"Well, you should have met some fine boy here in Thunder Canyon instead of going off to foreign parts like New Mexico," Tanya said wryly. But her eyes were sympathetic. "Why didn't you say something before now?"

She lifted her shoulder. Tugged the length of her ponytail over her shoulder, only to toss it back again. "I don't know. I guess...the more people I tell, the more real it is. And believe me, I felt like it was pretty real already."

Tanya squeezed her hand. "And it doesn't have anything to do with the fact your SUV was outside of the coach's house last weekend? Never mind. Your expression is plain enough." A loud commotion sounded near the front of the grill.

The team had arrived.

And despite Faith's intention to leave, she couldn't make herself do it.

She sat there, her vision pinpointing on the door as the players trooped in, one after another. Todd Gilmore had Erik on his shoulder and both of them ducked way down to get through the doorway.

Cameron and his assistant coaches came in last.

Faith's heart chugged.

In seconds, though, he was surrounded by a crowd of people, whooping and hollering and chanting.

"I have to go," she whispered to her friend. "I can't do this."

"If it feels wrong," Tanya murmured, "then you shouldn't." She leaned forward and hugged her quickly. "Question is, what feels wrong?"

Faith slid off her bar stool. She fumbled with her coat. She could go out through the kitchen. Cameron would never know she'd been there. She stepped behind a table. Scooted around a high chair that held a sleeping toddler.

Made it to the kitchen.

And looked over her shoulder.

It was *all* wrong.

Why could she swing on the end of a rope in a canyon if she had to, but not face up to the man who held her heart in his hands, whether he knew it or not?

She squared her shoulders.

Swallowed the panic that wanted to nip at her.

And turned around.

She made her way to the front entrance. The door was still open, and cold air swept in around the cluster of people surrounding Cameron. Faith slid her arms into her coat. Her heart was in her throat. She sidestepped, and there he was.

The smile was on his face. But it wasn't evident in his deep brown eyes.

And when he saw her standing there, she knew down in her very bones that *she* was the reason for that.

And it made her want to weep all over again.

She moistened her lips. Stepped a little closer. "Congratulations on the win." It seemed silly to offer her hand. And hugging him was too painful to contemplate. So instead, she pushed her hands in her coat pockets. "You're going to be a hero in this town for the next few decades."

"The kids are the heroes," he said smoothly. He

nodded at someone's laughing comment, then closed his hand over Faith's elbow. "Excuse us for a minute." He drew her outside onto the wooden sidewalk and let go of her the second they were clear of the doorway.

Faith swallowed, but the knot in her throat remained, nearly suffocating her.

"Are you going to hyperventilate if I ask how you're doing?" His voice was even. Cool.

She flushed. Shook her head. "I'm fine." Miserable, more like. "And…I'm sorry. For the way I ran out like that."

"Not a problem." His voice was as bland as it had ever been. "I got the message. I just wanted you to know that Erik's still expecting you to go tobogganing with him again. Your choice whether you do or not."

She felt as if he'd slapped her. "I have no intention of disappointing Erik."

His jaw cocked a little in the first indication that he wasn't as removed as he appeared. "Good." His gaze shifted past her. "Looks like Romano's gearing up to write some parking tickets. You should move your SUV before he gets to you." Then he turned and went back inside.

Faith shivered.

The walls inside The Hitching Post were bulging with townspeople. Friends. Co-workers.

Never in her life had she felt more alone.

Chapter Thirteen

One of the hardest things Cam ever did was to leave Faith standing on the sidewalk outside the grill.

But he couldn't stay there with her. He couldn't bear to see her hazel eyes glaze with panic if he so much as mentioned a future.

And now that *that* particular door had been opened inside him, he couldn't be around her and *not* think about the future.

So he walked into the restaurant where it felt stuffy and close because of all the bodies packed inside. He immediately spotted Erik. He'd moved on from Gilmore to Romance—who *had* gotten to play briefly that night and was, not surprisingly, trying to hog credit for a win that was rightfully owned by the entire team.

Cam left Erik be and headed to the bar. On his way, though, someone slapped a long-neck into his hand.

Good enough for him. The beer was cold and maybe, if he drank enough of them, he'd forget the stinging sensation inside his chest. Mayor Brookhurst appeared, looking as self-satisfied as he ever did. "Come on over here, Cam. Want to introduce you around. Have you met Caleb Douglas?" He gestured to a silver-haired man wearing a Stetson on his head and turquoise on his belt buckle.

Cam stuck out his hand. "Mr. Douglas. It's a pleasure to meet you. A person can't live in Thunder Canyon without having heard the Douglas name a time or two." Or twenty, since the man seemed to own half the town, and a lot of the land surrounding it. And for Cam, the greeting was automatic. A throwback to the days of schmoozing clients. But just because he'd retained the ability didn't mean he cared about the life he'd left behind.

Which was a revelation he owed to Faith.

Who couldn't face the notion of a future that included him.

"Fine game tonight," the man drawled, fortunately unaware of Cam's preoccupied thoughts. "Looks like your boy over there's recovered from his incident with my mine. Would've come by to see how he was doing myself, but I've been tied up with business. Understand my wife, Adele, went by the hospital, though. She assured me he was well on the mend."

"He was. And—" Cam looked over when he heard a crash of glasses. He wasn't even surprised when his son stood in the middle of the fracas, looking innocent. "As you can see, he's still keeping things lively."

Caleb's pale green eyes looked amused. "Nothing like a son." He settled his hat again. "Brookhurst here's been singing your praises, but I prefer to draw my own conclusions. Be looking forward to seeing your name on the ballot for council member. It's sometimes good to have new blood from people committed to this old town." He lifted his hand, acknowledging someone's hail. "I'm sure we'll be talking again," he said as he moved off.

Cam immediately headed for Erik, where one of the waitresses had already begun sweeping up the mess. He hooked his arm around his boy and lifted him clear.

"I wanna talk to Faith." Erik's overtired gaze was roving over the people.

"Not tonight. She's gone home."

"Da-ad!"

"You can call her tomorrow." And damned if he didn't envy his kid for that fact. "You might not need any sleep, but your old man does." Cam would first have to eradicate Faith from his thoughts in order to get some sleep, but he had no intention of sharing that particular nugget.

"I gotta get my basketball from Todd. He was gonna get all the guys to sign it for me." Erik squirmed out of Cam's grasp and headed for the knot of players that had commandeered several tables.

Cam watched him go.

"Congratulations on the win." Chris Taylor stopped next to Cam. "Next thing you know, the town'll be expecting you to do this during football season, too."

"Gotta get through baseball first." He didn't for a second believe Faith's brother just *happened* to be hanging around The Hitching Post for the post-game celebration. As far as Cam had been able to tell, Dr. Chris Taylor rarely did anything without purpose.

"Faith was pretty happy to hear you've got Erik starting up with the climbing. And that he's going to do Little League." The doctor made no effort at being subtle.

"She likes my son," he said neutrally.

"She loves *you*," Chris said flatly.

The sting in his chest was more like a wrecking ball plowing through him. "She has a funny way of showing it," he muttered. He didn't for a minute believe that Faith would've told her brother about the episode at his house, either. And just because he hadn't done anything about it just yet, didn't mean he didn't plan to.

Even above the raucous music and voices inside the grill, he could hear the doctor's sigh. "I'm gonna cut to the chase, here," the man said after a moment. "One, because I think you're a decent guy who—judging by the glare you're giving me—has fallen for my thick-headed sister. Two, because my damn pager is liable to go off any second again, and I'm gonna have to book."

"You don't have to cut to anything," Cam assured him, his voice tight. "When it comes to your sister, there's nothing I need to discuss." And "fallen" didn't begin to cover what he felt where Faith was concerned.

"Do you love her, or not?"

Cam's molars ached from his jaw clenching so

tight. "What does it matter? She's made her feelings clear."

"She ran scared, I suppose." Chris didn't look surprised. "And didn't bother to tell you why."

Cam's patience was nil. "Her reasons are her own." Erik had begun bouncing the basketball on the wooden bar. But before he could get over there, one of the waitresses whisked it away with a grin and replaced it smoothly with a bowl of ice cream.

A successful sidetrack maneuver.

"Ordinarily, I'd agree with you," Chris said. "But you know what? I'd like to see my sister be happy again. I thought she was on that track lately. Ever since Erik went down the shaft, anyway."

"Right. She adores my kid. I know."

"Man, you two are suited," the doctor muttered. "Yeah. Faith likes kids. Adores 'em. Which has made it pretty damn hard for her to adjust to the fact that she can't have any."

Cam jerked. "What?"

Chris shook his head. "What the hell do you two talk about when you're together? Or is it just a sex thing?"

Cam's fist curled. "Don't go there."

"Then try this one on for size, and I hope to hell it fits, 'cause when she finds out I'm talking about her business, I'm going to be in the doghouse with her, big time. Dammit." He pulled his pager out suddenly and peered at the display. "The bastard she'd been married to walked out on her about two days after she learned there were no medical miracles that would help her conceive. But Jess wanted kids as bad as she did. Only instead of dealing with the blow the way you'd expect after being married to someone for six years, he told her he couldn't waste any more time waiting for the impossible to happen, so he went out and got himself a woman who could provide them. *I* don't consider it a great loss. The guy never went out of his way to make Faith feel particularly special. Hell, she told me once the guy proposed in the drive-thru at a fast-food restaurant. Just handed over the bag of tacos with a 'wanna get married?' and that was it. No ring. No nothing. But…well, there you go. She still loved him."

"I'm *not* her ex-husband," Cam gritted. "And if she can't see that—"

"Maybe she just needs some help opening her eyes," the other man suggested. "So she can stop looking at the past and start looking at the future. Figure maybe you might know something about having to do that." He slid his pager back on his belt and headed for the door.

Cam frowned, watching the man depart. Then he exhaled and went over to collect his son. But Erik was still eating the ice cream, so Cam stood behind him at the crowded bar, waiting, while Taylor's words drummed inside his head. He stared at the painting of the Shady Lady. But he didn't see the curving limbs discreetly covered by some flimsy fabric.

He saw Laura. As clear as if she were standing in front of him. And she was smiling the same smile she'd worn the day of their checkerboard picnic—as if he'd done something particularly pleasing to her.

Then she turned, her black hair drifting.

And she was gone.

Okay, Laura. I heard you.

Cam's hand closed over Erik's shoulder. "Come on, son. Let's go home."

"I'm not finished with my ice cream." Cam hefted the boy up on his shoulder, and handed him the bowl. "We'll bring the bowl back later."

Then he carried his boy outside and they walked all the way back to the high school to collect his car.

They planned the entire while.

"Um, Blondie?"

It was Saturday morning and Faith was at the station putting the finishing touches on the budget for Jim. "Just a sec, Derek." After she got the paperwork out of the way, she was going to go see Cameron. She'd already told Jim that morning that she needed a few days off, and he'd agreed to cover her territory.

Maybe Faith had ruined things too badly for repair where her relationship with Cam was concerned.

But she couldn't get through another night without doing something. So if that meant taking the chance of him turning her away, or worse, that she'd gain his pity, then too bad.

Either way, she wasn't going to be any worse off than she already was.

And if she had to, she could use the few days off to fall apart.

God, she hoped she didn't have to.

She hoped she could make Cameron understand. That he wouldn't hate her for being so afraid, so—

"Yo. Faith." Derek's voice was a little more insistent. "Seriously. You might want to check this out."

She set down her pen and turned her chair to face him. "Check *what* out?"

Derek was standing at the windows that overlooked Main. He pointed. "Looks like the high school marching band out there."

Faith joined him. Sure enough. There was the band in the same style uniforms they'd worn when she'd attended school there, marching right down the center of the street heading in their direction. "Maybe it's because of last night's game. Winning the state championship."

"Didn't hear about any parade being planned," Derek countered. "They'd have had to have a permit. Fire would've been required to be on hand."

A few other men, still in their turn-outs from the call they'd just been out on, joined them at the window. One of them pointed. "Isn't that the coach?"

Faith nodded. Cameron walked alongside the band, but she couldn't see much more than his head from this angle. "Definitely because of last night's game." She wanted to press her nose against the windowpane, but made herself go back to her desk and the budget.

Telling herself she would go to Cam was one thing. Seeing the man before she'd expected to—though it didn't change her mind now that it was made up—made her feel positively weak in the knees.

And the last thing she needed was for Derek and his band of merry men to see just how female she could be. She'd never live down their ribbing.

It wasn't long, however, before she could hear the beat of the big bass drums and the pipe of the band instruments.

And she found herself looking toward the window despite her intentions otherwise. Looking, then getting back up, and moving over.

On the sidewalk outside the building, she could see a crowd was forming. People out enjoying the crisp, clear Saturday morning. A few police officers in uniforms. Cheryl Lansky, even, with her headset still in place and her phone cord dangling back toward the doorway of the police station.

The band had stopped moving down the street and was now marching in place.

"What's that they're playing?" someone asked.

"You are my sunshine, my only sunshine," Derek singsonged.

"Go back to baking," someone else told him and they laughed.

Faith's palms pressed flat against the glass. She could see Cameron far more clearly now, as he rounded the front of the band. He wore blue jeans and a charcoal gray shirt with a down vest over it, and his hair rippled a little in the faint breeze as he stopped to speak to the drum major.

Then Erik darted into view, his young legs pumping as he kept ahead of several members of the basketball team who jogged behind him. He held a flat box over his head and as she watched, Cam hastily reached over to rescue it before the boy dropped it.

The band kept playing.

And Cam turned to face the building.

Faith stood, rooted in place.

"What in the hell is that man doing?"

Faith barely heard. Her gaze was glued to Cam's face. He'd seen her through the window. No question. And her heart couldn't make up its mind whether to stall completely or beat as frantically as a humming-bird. Particularly when Cam and Erik walked toward the building, bypassing the gathering crowd.

"He's coming in here."

Faith followed Cam's progress through the window. He disappeared around the side of the building, and a moment later, came through the door.

The firefighters scattered like startled mice. Any other time and she'd have laughed herself silly at the sight of six large men trying to look casual and failing miserably.

Any other time.

Right now, she couldn't do more than stand there in front of the window, without a coherent thought in her head.

Cam pointed at a desk chair and Erik obediently sat and took the box back from his dad. He was grinning as if he'd just discovered a forgotten gold nugget in his pants from the mine shaft.

Then Cam walked right up to her.

She tucked her hands behind her back to hide the fact that they were shaking.

His brown gaze roved over her face, his expression assuring her he knew just what she was doing. "Maybe you better sit down," he said after a long moment. "In case you pass out or something."

She swallowed, pride stiffening her spine. For the rest of her life she'd probably never live that one down. The first and only time she'd ever hyperventilated. "Why would I pass out?"

"Because I'm gonna talk about the F word."

Her eyebrows shot up. "I *beg* your pardon?"

"The *future*."

Her lips parted. Emotion squiggled inside her. Hope. Fear. "What about it?"

He didn't even glance around at their audience. His gaze was focused only on her. "I want one. With you. I know this is fast. We haven't…dated. I haven't romanced you. And I won't push for more than you're ready for." His lips twisted a little. "I'll try not to push," he amended, gruffly. "But I know what you make me feel. And I'm done pretending that it's not happening. And I'm done pretending I don't like it. I love you. And I want you in my life. As my wife. My lover. My partner. My friend."

Her eyes flooded. "Cam, you don't know what you're taking on."

"A golden woman who can stand beside me until we're hunched over in rocking chairs, watching our great-grandchildren sled on the hill behind our house?"

The tears flooded over. Grief sucked hard at her, pulling her under. "That's just it," she whispered. And it didn't matter that she'd planned to talk to him later. The time was now. Avid audience or not. "I can't *give* you children."

His eyes were fiercely soft.

And unsurprised.

He stepped closer. Tilted his head lower toward hers and cupped her cheeks to catch her tears on his thumbs. "We already have Erik. And any more we might be blessed with may not come from *our* cells, but they'll come from our *hearts*. Come on, Faith. There's a world of children out there needing good parents, if and when we decide to add to our family. But the bottom line is that *you* are the one I need."

Oh, how badly she wanted to believe him. "That's easy for you to say now. But you haven't had any time to think about it."

"Your brother told me last night about the reason your marriage ended. And I didn't need any time then. But I wasn't going to show up at your door at one in the morning and casually suggest we get married. You think I'm gonna behave like your ex-husband did, but you're wrong from start to finish. You think you're not the kind of woman to inspire romantic gestures. And you're wrong there, too."

He closed his hands over her shoulder and turned her to face the window again.

The entire basketball team stood there, grinning like darned idiots. And every one of them held out a bouquet of roses. Red ones. White ones. Yellow. It was a veritable garden of them, right there in the middle of winter.

And behind them, the band was still playing that ridiculous song. "You are my sunshine," she whispered thickly and turned back to Cam.

"I'll spend the rest of my life romancing you, Faith

Taylor. Because you are *sunshine* in my life." His voice dropped. Turned fierce. "Do you understand me? You light up the corners. You're the one who's helped me see that what I have here in this town isn't only honoring someone's memory. It's a *life*. And it's good. And with you, it'll be all I've ever wanted. I'm not saying there won't be hurdles. Because there always are. But I'm saying we can take them together. You and me. And that terror over there who's even now spinning around on the office chair—" his voice rose so Erik could hear "—needs you, too."

"Is it my turn yet, Dad?"

"In a minute." Cam didn't look away from Faith's face. "Just give us a chance, Faith. I'm hoping the fact that I *could* make you nearly pass out last week means that this is really important to you, too."

She settled her hands tentatively on his chest. Even through the puffy down vest she felt the charge of his heart. "My *brother* told you last night?"

He nodded once. "I'd have come for you sooner or later, though. I couldn't have stayed away much longer. I thought there was only one thing I needed in this life, Faith. The knowledge that my kid was safe and happy. But there's something else I need now, too. And that's you."

"I was…going to come to you, too," she whispered. "I just…when Jess left it wasn't so much losing *him* that hurt. It was losing the dream of this marriage that was supposed to be as long and enduring as my parents'. But I knew if I were to ever lose you…I don't think I could survive it, Cam."

His breath hissed through his teeth. He leaned down. Kissed her hard. Briefly. "I'm not going anywhere, Faith. My future is here. With you."

Her fingers curled into his vest. She reached up and pressed her mouth to his. Softly. Lingeringly. Then she drew away and sucked in a shaking breath. "What's in the box?"

"What box?" His eyes were gratifyingly glazed.

She smiled a little, loving him so much her heart was cracking wide open with it. "The box that Erik's clutching."

"Right." He slid his palm around her neck, as if he needed to make sure she was going to stay put. He gestured at Erik and the boy gleefully hopped off the chair, only to nearly fall on his nose from all the spinning. But Derek caught him up and set him on the straight course toward them.

When he reached them, Cam flipped back the lid.

Inside was an enormous pink cookie.

"First homemade cookie we ever made," Erik said proudly. "I kinda blew up the mixer, though. Dad was pretty…um…anyhow, it's 'cause of Valentine's Day last week. I never got to tell you happy Valentine's Day."

Faith knelt down beside him, as much because her legs were going to give out as anything. She looked at the cookie.

We love Faith had been spelled out in uneven strokes of white frosting.

She ran her hand over Erik's head. "Nobody but my mom has ever baked a cookie for me before," she admitted.

He looked at her. "I could bake you a cookie every Valentine's Day, maybe."

And that was it. Her heart broke open the rest of the way. And she knew she'd never want to close it again.

Not as long as she had the Stevenson men to love.

"Maybe we'll bake them together," she suggested, laughing a little through the tears that clogged her throat. "See if we can *not* blow up any more mixers."

He suddenly threw his arms around her neck. Cam barely rescued the boxed cookie in time to save it from flying.

"Thanks for rescuing us," Erik whispered in her ear.

She hugged him back. "Thanks for rescuing *me*," she whispered.

Then she looked up at Cam. He drew her to her feet. "Is this a big enough display for you?" he asked gently.

Outside the window, the players were still standing with the roses. The band still played. Erik had sat down at her desk where Cam stuck the cookie and was busy tearing off a great huge corner of it as his avid eyes roved over the interesting aspects a fire station might hold.

Faith looked from all of it, back to Cameron's face. "I never needed a display." She slid her arms around his neck. "I just needed to believe."

"And do you?"

His eyes were dark. And just as vulnerable as Erik's.

"Yes," she said softly. Joyfully. Peacefully. "I believe. My future is with you, Cameron."

His lashes lowered for a moment. "Thank you."
Then his palms slid behind her and he hauled her close.
His mouth covered hers.
And it was *right*.

* * * * *

MONTANA MAVERICKS:
GOLD RUSH GROOMS
continues in March 2005 with
PRESCRIPTION: LOVE by
USA TODAY *bestselling author Pamela Toth*

Find out what happens when Thunder
Canyon's own Dr. Chris Taylor meets his
match in city-slicker Dr. Zoe Hart,
as gold fever rages in the background!
Available wherever Silhouette books are sold.

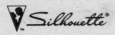

SPECIAL EDITION™

GOLD RUSH GROOMS

Lucky in love—and striking it rich—
beneath the big skies of Montana!

The excitement of Montana Mavericks: GOLD RUSH GROOMS continues

with

PRESCRIPTION: LOVE
(SE #1669)

by favorite author

Pamela Toth

City slicker Zoe Hart hated doing her residency in a
one-horse town like Thunder Canyon. But each time
she passed handsome E.R. doctor Christopher Taylor in
the halls, her heart skipped a beat. And as they began
to spend time together, the sexy physician became a
temptation Zoe wasn't sure she wanted to give up. When
faced with a tough professional choice, would Zoe opt to
go back to city life—or stay in Thunder Canyon with the
man who made her pulse race like no other?

Available at your favorite retail outlet.

Where love comes alive™

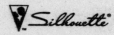

SPECIAL EDITION™

Don't miss the second installment in the exciting new continuity, beginning in Silhouette Special Edition.

THE FORTUNES OF TEXAS: Reunion

A TYCOON IN TEXAS

by Crystal Green

Available March 2005

Silhouette Special Edition #1670

Christina Mendoza couldn't help being attracted to her new boss, Derek Rockwell. But as she knew from experience, it was best to keep things professional. Working in close quarters only heightened the attraction, though, and when family started to interfere would Christina find the courage to claim her love?

Fortunes of Texas: Reunion— The power of family.

Available at your favorite retail outlet.

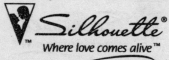

Where love comes alive™

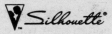

SPECIAL EDITION™

Introducing a brand-new miniseries by
Silhouette Special Edition favorite author
Marie Ferrarella

One special necklace,
three charm-filled romances!

BECAUSE A HUSBAND
IS FOREVER

by Marie Ferrarella
Available March 2005
Silhouette Special Edition #1671

Dakota Delany had always wanted a marriage like
the one her parents had, but after she found her
fiancé cheating, she gave up on love. When her
radio talk show came up with the idea of having her
spend two weeks with hunky bodyguard Ian Russell,
she protested—until she discovered she wanted Ian
to continue guarding her body forever!

Available at your favorite retail outlet.

Where love comes alive™

Curl up and have a

Heart to Heart

with

Harlequin Romance®

Just like having a heart-to-heart
with your best friend, these stories
will take you from laughter to tears
and back again. So heartwarming
and emotional you'll want to
have some tissues handy!

Next month Harlequin is thrilled to bring you
Natasha Oakley's first book for Harlequin Romance:

For Our Children's Sake (#3838),
on sale March 2005

Then watch out for....

A Family For Keeps (#3843),
by Lucy Gordon, on sale May 2005

Available wherever Harlequin books are sold.

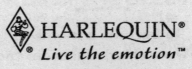

HARLEQUIN®
Live the emotion™

HRHTH

SILHOUETTE *Romance*®

TRADING PLACES WITH THE BOSS
by Raye Morgan
(#1759) On sale March 2005

When Sally Sinclair switched roles with her exasperating boss, Rafe Allman, satisfaction turned to alarm when she discovered Rafe was not only irritating…he was also utterly irresistible!

BOARDROOM BRIDES:
Three sassy secretaries are about to land the deal of a lifetime!

Be sure to check out the entire series:

THE BOSS, THE BABY AND ME
(#1751) On sale January 2005

TRADING PLACES WITH THE BOSS
(#1759) On sale March 2005

THE BOSS'S SPECIAL DELIVERY
(#1766) On sale May 2005

Only from Silhouette Books!

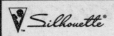

INTIMATE MOMENTS™

presents a provocative new miniseries by
award-winning author

INGRID WEAVER

PAYBACK

Three rebels were brought back from the brink and
recruited into the shadowy Payback Organization.
In return for this extraordinary second chance, they
must each repay one favor in the future. But if they
renege on their promise, everything that matters
will be ripped away...including love!

Available in March 2005:
The Angel and the Outlaw
(IM #1352)

Hayley Tavistock will do anything to avenge the
murder of her brother—including forming an
uneasy alliance with gruff ex-con Cooper Webb.
With the walls closing in around them, can love
defy the odds?

Watch for Book #2 in June 2005...
Loving the Lone Wolf
(IM #1370)

Available at your favorite retail outlet.